SPITEFUL PUNKS

DOLLS AND DOUCHEBAGS PART ONE

MADELINE FAY

Happy reading!

Madeline Fay

Copyright @ 2021 Madeline Fay
Spiteful Punks (Dolls and Douchebags Part One)
Dark, Bully, Why Choose Romance

First Publication: March 5th, 2021
Editing by Proofs By Polly
Cover by HQ Artwork
Proofreading by Emma Luna At Moonlight Author Services
Formatting by Inked Imagination Author Services

All rights reserved. Except for use in any review, the reproduction or
utilization of this work, in whole or in part, in any form by any electronic,
mechanical or other means now known or hereafter invented, is forbidden
without the written permission of the publisher.
Published by Madeline Fay

The unauthorized reproduction or distribution of a copyrighted work is
illegal. Criminal copyright infringement, including infringement without
monetary gain, is investigated by the FBI and is punishable by fines and
federal imprisonment.
Please purchase only authorized electronic editions and do not participate
in, or encourage, the electronic piracy of copyrighted materials. Your
support of the author's rights is appreciated.
This book is a work of fiction. Names, characters, places, brands, and
incidents are the products of the author's imagination or used fictitiously.
Any resemblance to actual events, locales or persons, living or dead, is
entirely coincidental.
This is a Dark, Bully, Why Choose Romance.

TRIGGER WARNING

This is a dark, bully theme, and enemies to lovers romance story ending with a cliffhanger. A why choose romance where the heroine won't have to choose between her different love interests.

This book contains graphic and violent scenes, including rape, physical and emotional violence, child abuse, swearing, sexual scenes, and PTSD. Suitable only for readers aged 18+.

Please do not take this warning lightly if you are sensitive to any of the triggers listed above.

This is part one of Spiteful Punks (Dolls and Douchebags), which does end with a HEA eventually.

If you have any issues regarding the book, please reach out to the author using one of the links on the last page.

Content updated on 03/15/2021

*"To all of the queens who are fighting alone
Baby, you're not dancin' on your own."*
~Ava Max~
True Queen.

PROLOGUE

Tillie

"Obedience is a funny thing. You don't catch on the first time right away, but I can guarantee that the second time around it will click as I teach you, beating it into your skin." His back is turned to me, the gypsy symbol patch of a Joker expanding on his MC cut, mocking me from my kneeling position on the cold, concrete flooring.

It doesn't matter how many hours my knees are in this position, time becomes an endless loop of agonizing pain, until it eventually numbs me inside and out like a shot of morphine. They say if you keep doing the same thing every single day, your body gets used to that routine in a matter of time. I'm at the point where my body is used to the feeling of being tormented. He always seems to know when I shut down everything around me, as I try to find my happy place, no matter how small. It must be the emotionless glint in my eyes, a faraway look that says nothing you can do really hurts me anymore. That's a lie though, a filthy lie that I keep speaking, screaming out just to prove I'm not weak. He comes up with new ways to torture me, to make the suffering last just before my breaking point. My body can't take much more, the burning inside of each cut is like salt rubbing into the wounds he inflicts upon me.

I must have spaced out because the next thing I know my head whips to the side with a searing pain across my right cheek, throbbing with my pulse. His dirty hand that reeks of cigarettes and engine grease grips the underside of my jaw tightly, bruising the skin there. A reminder he can do anything he wants and get away with it. He doesn't care if my face is bloody so long as I'm staring right into his soulless eyes.

A cough slips past my lips as he tightens his hold. Don't ask me why I needed to cough, I think it's just a way to suck in a new breath, oxygen I was denied from that brief second his hand connected with my face. This is why I can't get lost in my head, he senses it like a shark in the water and wants my full attention on him. The sick bastard gets off on my agony, it feeds him... his panting breath fanning my face in his excitement. Whiskey, cigarettes, and under all that is the stench of death. The smell alone has bile rising from my stomach to my throat. A man can only go so far in life without having the grim reaper attach to his wicked soul, knowing he's owned after doing countless deeds for the devil.

"Tillie, Tillie, you never learn." He pauses, his cracked lips stretched into a smile, and I'm sucking in a breath to avoid the vomit that so badly wants to pass my lips. "I'm going to give you one chance and if you can leave a mark on me, I'll let you run, girl until you're far, far away from here." I watch his lips form the words and it sounds so distant, I can hear every little sound around me but him.

He releases my jaw with a rough shove like he's disgusted with me. My breath stills in my chest with a whimper trying to escape as what he says registers in my head. My one eye that isn't swollen shut stares him down warily, afraid to believe anything that comes out of his mouth. Everything is always a test, a way to weaken me more with false hope. Escape is out of my reach, a tease that makes my throat dry and kills me slowly inside like a deadly cancer.

Hope.

Freedom.

All an unforgiving lie. Lies that burn off his tongue, slithering towards me until it bites into my skin and is worse than the torment he gives.

"That's right, swing at me with your frail, weak arms." He taps his chin three times in quick succession with his filthy finger. "Come on, with your best shot. Right here." His brown eyes, which are so familiar to my own if I were to stare into a mirror, harden into a glint I know so well.

Sometimes it's like looking into a bottomless pit and realizing there isn't a way out, staring right into the eyes of Satan.

My arms are weak, covered in scrapes and bruises, feeling like cement is holding me down. Do this, hit him with everything I've got, or suffer more punishment. My eyes squeeze tight, picking door number one because it's my best bet and I don't see another way out of this. When I was little, Uncle Rig would have tried his best to keep me away from his MC President because he noticed the evil his brother possessed. Payne took over for Grandfather when he passed away, the man is known for his cruelty and insanity. Unfortunately, he is also my Dad. Uncle Rig, Vice President of the club, first right hand man to Payne, did

3

everything he could to shield me from club business and the cruel world. That bubble popped suddenly, one day the sun was shining bright and the next I found out Uncle Rig was just gone. Disappeared without a goodbye and that was the day my heart knew I'd never seen him again. Two weeks after his disappearance was when my obedience lessons started with dear old Dad. That first lesson was three years ago.

The squeak of his leather cut jolts me out of my memories, making my eyes pop open wide, only to see darkness surrounding me as usual. I watch as Payne sits on his heeled biker boots, his chin jutting out, and pointing his index finger clad with rings towards his jaw for me to make a move. He's patiently waiting for my weak hit that I know without a doubt won't leave a mark. But I have to try.

Without thinking about it too much, I pull my arm back and take a driving swing that connects with his skin so hard that I know it hurts me more than it hurts him. Not even a flinch mirrors his face, but sweet satisfaction gleams in his cruel eyes at my display of weakness.

"Oh child, how I wish you were a boy instead of a pathetic cunt, and I'm betting you're wishing the same thing just about now. Don't you know men rule this big, bad world? Strength comes from a man, not a woman." He laughs in my face, spittle spraying everywhere and making me cringe away in disgust.

Demon Jokers are death, the devil's right hand in his dirty work, and makes God a laughing stock as they mock him with each deed the club delivers. All who know the Demon Jokers MC on the outskirts of Las Vegas fear them, but not as much as I do.

"Please, I'll do b-better! I promise!" My voice echoes in a cry of desperation.

I gasp on a tearful watery breath at the sound as it bounces off the cement walls that are stained in old splattered blood spots and other things I'd rather not think about. He slowly shakes his head in disappointment before straightening to his full height and walking over to the steel door that leads up the stairs into the club's bar area. My heart pounds in sync with his footsteps. He pauses at the door frame and looks over his shoulder at me with dark delight, which can only mean something is going to happen. Something that I'm not going to like.

"That's another funny thing, promises mean nothing unless you can prove it and I've only seen failure from you. You're going to find out what it means to be a woman in this world and spread your legs without a single word coming out of your whore mouth. You should have been opening your legs to many men for a long time now but I've been a good Father, no? Sixteen is the perfect age to lose one's innocence, don't you think?" He opens the heavy steel door with ease, his chuckle slowly eating away at me as the blood drains from my face when a group of the Joker's members fill the open space one by one.

The air has a smell that terrifies me. It reeks of disgusting lust that is aimed at my body and each Joker's facial expression tells me what's going to happen, no matter how loud I scream for help, it will be pointless in the long run. No one cares, no one will come, and I'm all alone.

Motorcycle boots shuffle over the cement basement floor and the sound of zippers lowering is like a gunshot going off in the silence. Sick, twisted eyes stare down at my crouched position as I hunch my shoulders in an attempt to appear smaller. It doesn't work for men like them, they have the same look of the Devil shining in their greedy, lustful gazes. The same look Payne has each time he sees me. It doesn't matter that I grew up around these men, some perched me on their knees and taught me my ABC's. It all comes down to this and any hope I was holding onto fades away as Cruz, the one guy I thought I meant something to, is the last to walk into the room.

"Do this, boy, and you're in. Training for the future President starts with this. You'll receive your patch afterward." Payne pats him on the shoulder, whistling as he climbs the stairs without looking back.

Cruz slams the door behind him with a carefree smile and his empty eyes take in the room, seeing me crouched on the floor like a wounded animal without a flicker of worry. Gone is the guy who showed any level of kindness to a young girl's heart. He may be a few years older than me but he played me for a fool as he charmed me into believing that love exists. The joke is on me. No love is shining in his eyes now. Instead, it's a dark and depraved gaze of a man with no emotions and abnormal thoughts. He's dead but oddly still breathing.

"Who's up first boys? I've been dying to claim this cunt for a while, she seems to think it's made of gold, such a tease and so very innocent... just the way I like them. So fellas, step in line because it's going to be a long wait!" Cruz says with a loud chuckle.

Ten Demon Jokers circle around me, gazing down at my shivering body and palming their hard dicks.

Poe taught me how to hold a shotgun at the age of five behind the junkyard the club owns.

Zagan's been beating the boys away from the doorstep since my body started blooming.

Nix, just last week was showing me how to tune up an old mustang in the garage.

Whiskey joked around and showed me how to slow

dance in a room full of bikers when I used to roam the club at night because I couldn't sleep with the loud music playing.

The list could go on and on of members who were always there for me growing up but right down to it... I'm nothing but their President's daughter, and that makes me hot off the press for picking with just one nod from their big boss. My dad's closest crew, guys I've known my whole life, roughly grab my legs to spread them open. Hands tear at my clothing as I kick, buck, shout, anything to get away, but it's useless as fingers tighten to hold me still. It doesn't do me any good as criminal eyes stare down at my exposed body with uncontrollable lust until I look away. My gaze catches on the ceiling, seeing the crooked nail, the imperfection, and for the next few hours, grunts sound in my ears, and pounds of my flesh is taken from me. My mind leaves to another place that isn't here, somewhere anywhere else but here. My screams never fade, they still echo in my head along with my sore throat that feels raw.

A sudden hit to my lip has me reeling back with the force, my face swinging to the side as the blow was delivered. Blood pools on that single split but I can't focus enough on why it doesn't seem to hurt. My body is moving without me controlling the movements, back and forth my back scrapes across the cold cement. I know one of the club members is grunting over my body, as he pushes inside me, I don't bother to look. It's as if I'm not really here, even though I can feel whoever is inside me with each dry thrust causing me unbearable pain. That hurts, having someone shove their way inside of your body when it's dry. That's when my own haunted screams reach me, breaking past the barrier I tried building around myself until it's over. Being tossed around like a rag doll, touching me in places I've never thought of being touched with my innocence that is no more. Payne was right, this is a man's world and I'm feeling the effects of it.

Someone tosses me onto my stomach, my body limp, and not really mine anymore at this point. I wish I could keep staring at that nail, to see something that will keep me partially sane. A hot breath bears down on my ear just as something small, sharp, and cold is placed on my back. My focus sharpens to that one object while my whole body tenses up after what feels like hours of having loose limbs.

"You're going to feel this, remember this, and you can't escape me after this. Tell me, Tillie, have you ever dreamed of your ass getting fucked?" Cruz chuckles just as he starts carving something into my shoulder blade.

My screams aren't screams anymore, they're howling prayers for the devil to come already and take my battered soul away. After some point he stops carving my skin, breathing heavily on top of me and giggling like a schoolgirl when the rest of the men clap in loud applause at his artwork. Every breath is like my last but it stops altogether when something hard touches between the line of my butt cheeks, somewhere a girl my age considers forbidden. Searing, unbelievable pain is all I can feel after that. A small, quiet voice reaches me and it makes me jolt as I realize it's me repeating the same thing over and over out loud.

"Please, God, let it end. Just let it end."

I must have blacked out at some point or I could have been wide awake the whole time but not really seeing anything because once again I'm staring up at that crooked nail. The sound of the basement door slamming shut with their echoing laughs makes my cold, stiff body start to shake as reality comes back like a splash of cold water. I wish it didn't. My mind is broken, beyond repair, and any inno-cence I possessed is long gone.

Laying here in the dark shivering, my body feels like it's made of stone and lead. Bleeding from wounds that have long healed over, buried so deep inside my soul that even I don't want to look but they seem to keep deeply cutting open. *Filthy, dirty, never clean,* keep repeating through my head as the semen between my thighs and every exposed part of my body starts to dry. I wish I could scrub it away with bleach, and as much as I try, tears can't form in my eyes. I'm all cried out and everything is numb inside until it comes crashing down as I try to sit up with a groan. I catch myself on my palms, my arms trembling and everything is blurry as if looking through a haze of smoke. My body jolts with a cry escaping my mouth when a hand lands on my shoulder but the weak, pathetic cry cuts off when I notice the sweetbutt crouched in front of me, eyes filled with rage and pity. Doris. She is like the mother hen of sweetbutts for the club, been around for years, and yet never once tried to leave. Maybe she has no place else to go like me.

"I have you, Tillie, I'm going to help you up and we're going to take one step at a time. When we walk out that door, don't you dare look down, and chin up no matter what happens. Don't give them that fear and each painful step will give you strength." She puts her arm around my waist and helps me towards the door, not once grimacing as I cry out with each shuffle of my feet.

I can't go through that door, monsters wait for me in leather vests. Blaring music comes from the other side of that steel door, sweetbutts getting dicks wet even with my smear of blood still coating club members' dicks, like it's a normal Saturday night. But it's not a regular day for me, it's

9

the day I lost one part of me I thought I would be able to give away when I was ready.

Ripped away.

Torn.

Just gone.

Bikers wait for me to do a walk of shame I have no control over with excited breaths that will just grow deeper as they take in their masterpiece of work.

"One day you'll get out of this hell hole. I'm going to help you soar so high that the only thing these bastards will see is the faint glint of your wings just as they kiss the sun. It's so close, I just need you to wait a little bit longer. I'm going to teach you what it takes to bring a man to his knees and have him crawling. Those who are patient, waiting to receive the sweetest revenge, are the ones who send the hounds from the depths of hell at their heels and see the world burning around you as a smile blooms on your face," Doris says in a hard voice, making me want to believe that not everything is shadowed in black and one day I'll see more than what is in front of me now.

She opens the door to the stairs, a sealed tight promise clear in every word, but the thing about promises is that they don't last forever.

The question is... do I stand tall or fall to my knees until I have nothing left to give anymore?

CHAPTER 1

Tillie

*Y*ou would think that I would get used to the music, the lights, the smell of spilled alcohol seeping through the dirty linoleum floors, and smoke lingering in the air, but I never do. The smell still turns my stomach with each small inhale. Luckily for me, the color of flashing strobe lights across my face blind me from seeing anything beyond the stage, making it almost bearable, and blocking out the view of eager men sitting before me. Hoots and drunken clapping fill the space as dollar bills fall onto the stage like confetti just as I jump up and grip the pole near the top with both hands to perform a fireman spin. The back of my right leg clenches the shiny, slippery metal as I swirl around seductively. My calf muscle burns from the grip I have on the pole as I descend to the stage floor, my neck arched back and my hair almost grazing the floor when I slide down slowly.

Just as Cardi B sings through the speakers *'Oh he's so*

handsome what's his name', my long, slender legs touch the ground, ending the song in the splits, my seven-inch platform stilettos glittering in the lights. Sweat coats the back of my neck making my long, brown hair curl at the ends and all I can hear is the ringing in my ears, my chest heaving after that grand finale.

"That's right, baby! Shake that ass!" Some random guy shouts, laughing when his friends make catcalls.

Faceless, drunken, rowdy strangers reach out to grab me with their filthy hands but I'm already heading towards the stage exit in a slow stride. The yearning to run always hits me hard after each time I'm on stage. If I broke into a jog, it would get me attention I don't want or need. Sometimes I wish my body wasn't curvy, that my five foot seven didn't make my legs look shapely and long. That my body would have stopped growing mid-teens, instead of growing breasts that drew every guys' eyes there, and a bubbly ass to make my Latina side stand out. Slightly big breasted, round ass, slender waist, and legs for days brought me attention I have never wanted. What it means to be a woman, the attention you get when you least want it.

Jimmy, the money grabbing sleazeball, comes out of the darkened corner left of the stage and has a broom in his hand to sweep up the rest of the flying dollar bills when I am finally able to step off the platform behind the curtain. I don't bother collecting any of the money I've earned with my body. It all just goes to the Joker's club members, I never see a dime and am only allowed the necessary items, like for instance the skimpy outfit I'm wearing tonight or my tennis shoes that are being held together with duct tape. I'm basically on display, lined up under the lights like a meat market and it's only a matter of time before I'm sold into the right greedy hands that Payne approves of.

My hands shake uncontrollably as I step into the dressing room and head right to the vanity just before my shaking legs collapse under me. I sit down on the small stool, staring at my reflection under the bright bulbs and grimace in the mirror at my caked face. Scrubbing viciously on one side of my face like I'm trying to peel a layer of skin away, I wipe the coats of foundation off that I'm demanded to wear. Seeing the stranger looking back at me, it's me but it's not. Who is the girl with one side of her face fresh, natural, and the other side hiding behind heavy coats of powder with red stained lips? I can't let myself stare too long at my face because rage always consumes me without knowing who the hell I am. I see a girl with a heart shaped face, wide lips with a small indent in the middle, high cheekbones from her father's side along with a natural-born tan skin, smooth as whiskey, but littered from the neck down with deep scars inside and out. The worst of my scars that were inflicted onto my body over the years are now covered up with tattoos. Can't have a girl roaming the school hallways with scars covering her body, too many people asking questions and it all comes back to me with a beating from dear old Dad.

Tattoos make more sense for someone like me because it's expected with my background. Everyone at school knows where I come from, it doesn't go unnoticed that I'm always surrounded by men in vests and bikes. It's another reason why I don't have friends. They go running in the other direction even when I keep my head down, fear stretched on their faces from being within walking distance of me. Appearing to be a normal girl during the day and stripper at night is like living with roommates. Bravo to Payne because he got what he wanted. A walking vessel with no one to turn to. My wide, dark brown eyes say one thing in the mirror when I look back at my reflection but they're screaming at me to run, to find a new life before it's too late. Calling to me, telling me to just get up and leave, and never look back, but where would I go?

I'm so deep in thought, trying to find the girl who has a glimpse of something, anything, living inside her that I nearly jump out of my body when a hand grips my shoulder, jagged nails digging into my skin.

"A lady never shows her true face so put that fucking makeup back on." Mom sneers down at me as she leans over my shoulder and grabs the tube of bright red lipstick, sitting down next to me on another stripper's vanity seat.

She grabs my chin forcefully and twists the lipstick cap off, forcing the tube of red back on my full lips with a trembling hand that shows signs of years of hard drug use as it eats away at her. She does the same thing, grabs foundation, swiping it across my face without looking me in the eye.

"Lorrie, I'm done for the night. I just put on my last show until next Tuesday. I have school in the morning." My voice comes out calm and reasonable even though on the inside I'm scared like a newborn baby with its first thunderstorm.

Lorrie, Mom, the lady who birthed me is a cold hearted bitch who happens to be a snitch. She always has great pleasure when she reports back to my dad with every little thing I do, even though she would like nothing better than to pretend I don't exist. It was bad enough when I was a kid, having to figure out how to survive on my own while she was snorting cocaine up her nose with the dollars she used to earn on stage.

"You're done when I say you're done. Next song is on in five after CeCe, don't disappoint me, Tillie. If only you were beautiful, you would be making more money and spending less time on the stage." Her words used to cut me deep every time but now they only leave a small mark that gets easier to brush off.

I'll never understand what I did for her to despise me so much, maybe it's because I was born in the first place? All I can remember growing up is her staring down at me with a disgusted look on her make-up coated face as if I was a constant reminder that she had a child to take care of. She may be a mom but she doesn't have the warming love of a mother for a daughter to back it up. Hell, I don't even look like her, I resemble that sick monster I call Dad. It's been two years since that night in the basement, where they tore me into pieces and fed my flesh to the wolves. She never once came to my rescue even when my screams could be heard from a mile away. I'll always remember the slow smirk that overcame her face when Doris and I made it to the top stair. Her gaze was all too pleased as she perched on Payne's lap, looking me up and down like I was the filth beneath her shoe. I felt like it too after that night, no matter how many times I showered. Every limp and drag of my feet felt like stones being tied to my ankles and haven't been cut loose since then. To say I hate this woman is an understatement. The reminder she likes to throw in my face that I'm just like her and will end up the same makes my heart race and wonder if there's a way out of this life before I really do turn into her.

"So young, such soft skin, absolutely glowing." Her shaking hand smoothes down my cheek before scratching her nail over the same spot causing it to sting and draws a droplet of blood. "But that will change soon. Very soon. I've been waiting for this day for forever." She has this slight glint in her eyes that makes my hands sweat because she only ever looks this excited when she's snorting coke or taking a needle to her vein.

"Waiting for what?" My voice comes out in a scared whisper but I know she hears me over the pounding music because her red rimmed eyes show just how poisonous she is. They sparkle with joy and have me leaning back in my seat to put distance between us.

Without another word, she stands, adjusts her boobs in her skin tight tube top that she really shouldn't be wearing at her age, and walks away without a backward glance. Leaving dread in the pit of my stomach and making me second guess everything. None of my dad's men have tried anything like they did that night in the basement but my mouth has been silenced a handful of times to put me in my place. I can work a pole like it's nobody's business, seduce a man with a quirk of a smile, and without desiring it... I can suck a cock until a man is pleading to God and coming within seconds. I've been cornered and groped without permission, shoved to my knees before a man, lost a lot of dignity, but haven't been pinned down by anyone since that night. The Prez hasn't allowed it and I don't know why that scares me but it does. I feel like I'm constantly waiting, looking over my shoulder for the ball to drop. I see the way the Demon Jokers stare at me like it's only a matter of time before they do it again. It's what keeps me in place, scared to live, and breathing out a single word that will only lead to me getting raped again by just a small lift of the Joker's President's pinky finger.

The beatings still happen repeatedly like Sunday church, an obedient bone will never be in my body and I think I rebel on purpose just so I can have some control over my life and feel a spark of something from disobeying orders. I sometimes think just taking a blade to my wrist will stop it all, but that's not my ending. I want to leave this place one day on my terms, not because I was forced to. Somehow,

I just know with my bastard dad, my time is running out, and with how my mom looked like a kid on Christmas morning just now... I'm going to wake up so broken beyond repair one day that I'll just be an empty shell. It's the same dreadful feeling I had two years ago in that basement.

Whistles and loud laughs of men bounce off the walls when the next song comes on. My cue to get back out there and smile until my cheeks hurt. I bite back a groan when 'Bad Things' comes over the speakers. This isn't a True Blood episode and this song always makes the men get even crazier out there. Learning to dance from Doris, I've worked that pole like my life depended on it because it does. It's either dancing for Hazards Strip Club, owned by the Demon Jokers, or being passed around like someone offering a joint to all the one percenters again because they won't refuse a chance to get a high from me.

Dropping to my knees at the entrance of the curtains, I start crawling towards the edge of the stage in slow movements with my back slightly arched, flipping my hair while biting my lower lip. I hate this. Nothing is hidden, I wish I could be dressed in my favorite leggings and oversized sweater that is stuffed in my locker, it brings me comfort.

Instead, I parade around in lacy underwear that I'm forced to wear and it doesn't leave anything to the imagination, all my past bared to the world as horny men gaze at me as if I'm an object and not a person. I love to dance, don't get me wrong, but only if it's something I want to do in a carefree way. Not this way. It's supposed to be sensual and exotic how my body moves but it just makes me feel dirty with all the predator eyes on me.

With a few hair flips, the front row drunks try reaching out to touch me with eager fingers but I slide back on my knees until my front is facing away from them so I don't have to look into their greedy eyes. With a couple of hip rotations and an eye roll that I know no one can see, I slowly start to bend backwards until my back touches the floor with my legs spread in the air and my body arched off the sparkly black stage. Usually, I'm pretty good at ignoring the gazes on me but I feel one that sends body wracking chills over me. It's kind of like someone spilling acid down my spine. Tipping my head back, my back arched so it looks like I'm in the throes of passion when in reality it's completely fake, I see a pair of cold, vacant blue all-too-familiar eyes staring me down from the edge of the stage.

Cruz.

The man that made me bleed when I didn't want to give him an ounce, a man I once found handsome standing at six feet tall, broad shoulders like he would protect me from anything that came my way. Little did I know he would ruin me, he became my villain when I needed a hero.

My heart stops beating for a second and it's like he knows because a snail-like smile takes over his face, showing the devil looking back at me. He never comes here, always doing the bidding of Payne without argument like a good little soldier, and hardly looks at me when my father is around, while I try to stick to the shadows at the compound. He always stands too close when we're alone in the same room, sneaking in touches that feel snake-like but he hasn't done anything else for two years, just torments me with words instead of actions. Right now, he's gazing at me like I'm no longer a person, as if I'm owned.

His.

I break eye contact, climbing to my feet, stumbling in my exotic heels towards the pole on shaking legs, and cursing myself for showing weakness. Bile crawls up my throat, pooling in my mouth and I'm counting down how much longer until the song ends. Twenty more seconds. If I run, it's only going to be reported back to Payne and I'll end up on my knees in that fucking cold basement with more scars dragging down my body. I'm going to run out of exposed skin one day. I should have listened to Uncle Rig when he told me to stay away from Cruz. His exact words still play on repeat in my head to this day,

"That boy, something isn't right with him in the head, Tillie, and you stay away from him because a man without a soul is only good at one thing. Not feeling a damn thing."

I remember it so clearly, sitting on the leather seat of his motorcycle, playing with the handles as he worked under the hood of a GT350. He would always glare at Cruz whenever he was around especially when I started growing boobs. I should have fucking listened when I was fourteen, I could have avoided him like the plague even if it wouldn't have changed a thing, at least the thought of preparing myself would have made it better for me. It took me having my body violated by Cruz to realize what monster lays beneath.

When the song ends, my feet can't carry me fast enough off the stage. Bypassing my vanity without stopping to wipe off my makeup, I head straight to my locker and swing it open so hard that it bangs against the metal locker next to mine. Not bothering to even change out of my underwear that sticks to me like a second skin and glitter covering me from head to toe, I quickly shimmy into my skinny jeans and my green sweater that hangs off one shoulder while slipping my feet into my converse in hurried movements. Grabbing my bag from the bottom, I shut the locker door and jump back with a shout stuck in the back of my throat.

"Tillie, you weren't trying to run away from me were you?"

CHAPTER 2

Tillie

"*C*ruz, I didn't see you-u there." My gulp is noticeably loud in the quiet of the changing room and his predatory eyes don't miss a thing as they narrow on the sweat dripping down my temple. "I was just leaving for the night, my shift is over. I have school in a couple of hours so I'm heading back to the compound." Why does my voice have to come out shaky and scared? He takes a deep breath through his nose and his eyes close in sick bliss, thriving on my fear.

Cruz is a sociopath and I'm wondering how I never saw it years ago when my heart throbbed for him. The crazy was right in front of me the whole time.

My pulse is jumping out of my body and trying to get the hell out of here, I only wish I could follow it instead of being trapped in this room with one of my worst nightmares. As far back as I can remember Cruz was always in my life. We grew up in the club together after the Demon Jokers took him off the streets. Payne found him wandering from dumpster to dumpster as a runaway and for some reason, my father took him under his wing. I'll never understand why. Cruz was a constant shadow of mine, around every lurking corner, and my silly, foolish heart thought he had a crush on me... I never saw the possessive ownership, not once, until it was too late. Every memory I have, Cruz takes a big place in it since the moment he stepped into the compound. From when Uncle Rig brought home my first crotch rocket at age fourteen, Cruz stood right behind me with hunched shoulders and his hands in his pocket as I tried to figure out how to balance my body on the damn thing. Yeah, that was pretty young for a girl to be riding around the streets alone and without a license but rules don't apply to people who deal in the criminal world. It was all an act just so Cruz could gain my father's approval, a father he never had... he could fucking have him for all I care. Payne and him were two peas in a pod, it used to make me jealous of the attention I didn't have but now... the fuckers can have each other for all I care.

The feel of him currently breathing on my face causes a shiver of dread down my spine. He lifts his hand, reaching around me, and trails it over my exposed shoulder blade, across the tattoo that covers the worst of my nightmares. The ridged letter C was carved into my right shoulder blade with a small swiss army knife by the asshole in front of me and yeah, it's not a small scar. It took a while to create, what he likes to call artwork, through my delicate skin. I had the needle stinging into my skin the first chance I got to cover it up, a feather covers the rigid bumps. It's not noticeable now but we both know what lays under the ink. My memories I'll have to carry with me always and to Cruz, it just means ownership. His property and a sick reminder for him.

"Why do you show your body to other men like you

want it? I bet you try fucking all those boys at that school of yours, but they know not to touch what's mine, don't they, little bird? Does the slut inside of you enjoy it?" His grip on my shoulder digs in the angrier he gets and I know I'm going to have a bruise right over his scar he takes pride in.

I slap his hand away and his eyes darken until it's only his pupils taking over the white of his eyes, his cheeks turning red in rage. Next thing I know my back is scraping against the cold metal lockers as he shoves his body against the front of mine and slams his fist repeatedly on the locker right by my head. The need to flinch is strong but I turn my head to the side because looking at him takes me back to that night. The smell, the fear, and the hopelessness all come back with him this close.

"No-o, Cruz, I wouldn't do that. No one compares to you." My words come trembling out on a lie that I hope he doesn't notice and my vision gets blurry around the edges, I keep blinking to get rid of it without looking at him still.

"Look at me!" He shouts in my face, spittle landing on my cheek, and his voice rings in my ears, causing a small whimper to escape from me.

My throat moves with a rough swallow, stalling to gain the willpower to gaze into his lifeless eyes. Once he has my attention again, he clears his throat, stepping back like nothing ever happened, and slicks back his greased up dirty blonde hair as if he didn't just have an outburst of rage.

"That's good to hear, little bird. The thought of anyone taking what's mine again makes me jealous. You know, I think about that night a lot. Sliding between those creamy thighs that tempt me every day and hearing your screams of pain can really do things to a man. Tell me you think about me too." It's not a question, it's a demand and by the faraway look in his eyes and a secret, sickening smile, he really is reliving that night.

Do I think about him? Yes. Every single fucking day because I'm equal parts terrified of him and at the same time I'd like nothing better than to take his swiss army knife and cut him into tiny pieces. That would take a long time but I'm willing to get the job done to satisfy my thirst for revenge. My father was right though, men do rule the world. The thing about that is when a woman hurts so deeply, she always gets her vengeance and one day I will too, even if I die trying.

"Of course, I think about it every night, Cruz. How could I forget?" I say with an almost bored tone and keep my expression blank but my nails leave marks in the palm of my hands from squeezing my fist tightly.

Like I could ever forget, all I feel is rage coursing through my blood. They say blood is thicker than water but I call bullshit. My own blood causes me to live in fear day in and day out, turning me into someone who has a taste for sweet retaliation pooling in the back of my throat that I almost choke on daily.

"That's a good thing about memories, you always have a reminder of them to look back on. I have to go, meeting with Payne about a special subject that I can't wait to get my hands on. I'll be seeing you, Tillie." He crooks his head, watching my pulse jump in my neck before leaning forward and placing a kiss there.

Those two seconds seem to last for a lifetime, but it's easier to breathe when he steps back from me.

He straightens his leather Joker vest with the prospect patch missing in its usual spot, his rings gleaming in the dim lighting. He winks at me before turning around and walking away without the fear of me stabbing him in the back.

The second he's out of sight, my legs collapse beneath me with my breathing shallow as the fear and memories resurface. I live in a bubble where I pretend it never happened, but every time I stare into the Joker members' faces, it's like they stick a needle into my bubbled world until it explodes and I'm out in the open just to be hurt again.

My head bangs against the locker behind me as I stare up at the ceiling through my tears that won't fall. How can a person heal when it's a constant reminder that you've been violated and passed around like a rag doll? When you see those people daily? Sometimes I think death is a better way, just take a small blade to my wrists and drift away but my body would be left alone as a hard shell that my soul was just keeping as a bodysuit. I think that pain would travel with me no matter where I go and it won't end with me leaving for good. I'd rather see this to the end where the compound goes up in lights, in a fire of explosion as it reflects back in my eyes.

One day.

Running my trembling hands through my hair, I sigh in frustrated defeat just before standing up and grabbing my bag off the floor when I head to the back of the building to leave. The need for an adrenaline rush grips me tight, making my skin itch. I need to have control and racing sounds like the perfect opportunity to ground me.

The exit sign ahead is like a beacon and I'm jogging down the hallway to get out of the strip club, my eyes dart to every hidden dark corner just in case I need to break into a sprint before hands can grab me. Slamming open the back door, the parking lot is lit with one lamp post, and my baby is parked right under the spotlight in all its glory. Shiny black and purple accents make my bike stand out but also blend in just like me. The only freeing moment I have in my life is when I'm riding down the streets with her between my legs. We live for that daring moment where all possibilities are endless and it's the danger I can control as I speed with my knees almost kissing the pavement. My crotch rocket is the only thing that gives me the illusion that all is going to be okay.

Fifteen minutes later, I'm pulling onto a long stretch of a deserted road with cars parked on the sides, their head-beams acting as a runway on either side of the pavement. My eyes scan behind the tinted visor of my helmet for Manny, the one and only money holder for the races, the guy you want to know when a race is happening. I met him a year ago when he followed behind me one night when I was feeling extremely daring on my bike and he hopped out of his car, dropping to his knees begging for me to race into the night. So here I am, waiting for a thrill and wanting to challenge a fucker to feel something.

Spotting Manny crowded by girls in tiny shorts and tube tops while he counts hundreds in his hands, he nods his head at me and points over to the other two cars lined up at a starting line. A tingle starts at the base of my spine and I pull out two hundred dollars from my bra so he sees that I'm in before tucking the money away again. I'm lucky enough to have this much on me, each earning is mine from crossing that finish line and somehow no one has found out about my addiction to racing or the money.

Easing up between a Mitsubishi and a Mustang, the two guys look over at the same time as the rumble of my engine rolls up. Easy grins light up their faces because they think I'm just a silly girl playing with the big guys but this is what I'm good at. Taking chances when every little aspect of my life is controlled, I make them eat the asphalt. I don't look the part of racing, a girl alone at night only dressed in a sweater and skinny jeans but what they don't know is I have nothing to lose. I'm all in.

"I think you're in the wrong playground, little girl!" Douche number one shouts out his window, slithering his gaze up and down my body. "But don't worry, baby, I got just the right jungle gym for you to play on." He gestures to his body, patting his lap which only causes me to roll my eyes.

"No, baby. Papi will take good care of you. Hop on off that bike and onto my cock," douche number two says, revving his engine while he laughs and grabs his dick through his pants.

I return my attention back to the road, twisting my bike handles to rev my own engine, shutting their mocking voices out. Manny swaggers out to the side while pulling out a bandana from his back pocket, winking my way and shaking his head at the two idiots mouthing off on either side of me. My tires squeal, kicking asphalt up and leaving a skid mark just as the bandana touches the ground.

This is all I have so I'm here for this, to win and show that I'm still breathing even when I'm being held under water.

Parking in the back of the compound, I shut my bike off and listen to the overly loud music coming from inside. The gate slams closed, my cage squeaking shut of rusty chains, causing the ground to vibrate from my toes and up to settle in my heart. I'll always park in the back near the junkyard and close to the garage because at least if I'm ambushed I can play in the maze of cars to hide even though it doesn't do me good in the long run. The garage holds special memories for me with Uncle Rig, he's the reason for my love of cars and anything that goes fast. The grizzle grump loved his bike like it was his own child but there was just something about tuning up an engine under a hood of a classic beauty or the excitement of seeing a vehicle you never thought you'd be standing next to.

Nothing like feeling the engine underneath you, the vibrations making your heart race just before you drop the clutch and take off like the devils hot on your heels. If Payne found out I've been street racing late into the night after my shifts, he'd most definitely take away my bike and lock me away in a room without windows to see the light of day again or starve me for a week straight. It could be a lot worse for me. He doesn't question why it takes me longer to make it home but maybe he doesn't care or notice because he's high on drugs or with his latest whore. I guess I can count myself lucky for that small miracle. Doesn't matter if I'm the best, the fastest, the most determined because I'm just a girl with heat between her legs.

I won tonight with extra cash in my bra and I won't give up doing this because I'm still feeling alive even if it's going to fade away soon. It's the only risk I'm willing to take and I've won money but not enough to stay off the streets when I decide to make a run for it. I just have to keep going until it is enough.

The real question is when will it be enough? There's only so much a person can take before they shatter like a bullet through a windshield. I haven't yet but I've been pretty close over the years. When the darkness creeps in like a lost lover, it kind of sticks to you like glue until you peel it off in each slow strip. I just haven't found a way to cope with everything, maybe I never will.

Taking off my black helmet, I swing my leg over the bike

while grabbing my bag before heading inside. Opening the back door, hard rock music blasts my ears, and the loud laughter of drunk or high members gets louder the more I walk down the hallway towards the main bar area. I keep my head down, hoping to go unnoticed until I can reach my room upstairs above the bar area.

"Slut," a sweetbutt mutters as she passes me with a tray of drinks, bumping my shoulder.

"Little Whore, why don't you get over here and join our party on your knees?" Whiskey shouts from his spot in the corner, his cock out and his hand in a club whore's hair as he shoves her down on him while she gags.

This is a typical night, the drinks flowing, cocaine lined on trays passed around and open fucking. Just seeing his dick plagues me with memories of him shoving inside me with his drunken laughter while he smacked my face around. I look away quickly which only causes him to bark out a laugh at my expense. Maybe his dick will fall off from a slow, painful disease.

My feet skid over the wooden floor, trying to bypass the bodies without touching anyone and I can see the doorway leading upstairs. Just a few more feet. It's been like this for two fucking years. The fear every second of every night, trying to live without giving in to death that creeps to my door or the way out of collapsing into the drugs that are passed around like candy here. Just as my foot touches the stairs, my name is being called by the devil himself from across the room. I wonder if ignoring him, he'll go find someone else to torment?

"Tillie." The warning is clear in his voice. "Come."

My grip tightens on my helmet, wondering if I swing hard enough if I can bash his brains out but he's too much stronger.

I'm weak and he knows this.

Turning around, I shuffle over to him through the sea of parting Demon Jokers with a bored expression even though I'm screaming inside with a cry of terror. I glance into a pair of eyes that tell me to keep my cool.

Doris is sitting on Payne's lap, stroking his arm but her posture is stiff the closer I get until I'm right in front of him. His eyes shift to my hand with the death grip on my helmet and smirks like he knows my thoughts but knowing I'll do nothing about it. He leans back, stroking his greying beard as he stares at me, thinking about something that I'm not going to like.

"Get on your knees girl." His tone is hard, demanding, and he points at the floor near his boots.

My knees lock into place for a second, his brown eyes narrowing before I resolve and sink down until my skin touches the floor. I wish I could say this is the first time someone has told me to get on my knees but it's not. I've been violated too many times in the darkest corners... Those aren't broken rules as long as I'm not getting fucked. Cruz says that's only for him now but says some things I could learn from and my fucking father agrees. For once the club goes quiet, waiting to see what's going to happen but you can still hear someone getting their cock sucked in the background along with my heavy breathing. My eyes stray to the floor near his scuffed up boots until his next words stop my heart altogether.

"Do you think of me as an idiot? That I wouldn't find out?" His voice is low as he tsks me and swiftly kicks his leg out, shoving his boot onto my chest causing me to fall backwards with my back smacking sharply on the floor. "Answer me!"

His boot comes down on my chest once more as he

stands in one fluid movement to loom over me, making it hard to breathe.

"Find out what, Payne?" I manage to rasp out, but I already know what he's talking about.

He knows.

"Haven't I given you everything? Do you want for nothing?" He moves his boot away, allowing me to draw in a proper breath before crouching down to run his finger over my brow.

I shrink away from his touch with a flinch, my vision tunneling as I see more booted feet crowding closer. It's too much. No! It's happening again! At this point, I'm gasping with every inhale and my lips tremble in terror. Payne snaps his fingers in front of my face to bring my focus back on him. He's smiling like my fear pleases him which no doubt it does.

"I want for nothing." My whisper is low, only he can hear that causing him to chuckle as he straightens up from his crouched position.

"Exactly, imagine my shock when a little birdy told me that you've been sneaking around at night." He goes to sit back down, dragging Doris onto his lap again even though Lorrie is his sweetbutt, practically his old lady.

I guess none of that matters in this lifestyle. You're a whore on the outside and inside to these guys, Lorrie's probably blissfully riding on a cocaine high right about now as she fucks some other Joker.

My mind runs a mile a minute before it clicks. Cruz followed me, I shouldn't have been so careless after seeing him back at the strip club.

I'm fucking fucked. So stupid of me, I shouldn't have gone.

I peel myself off the floor, sitting up with a hiss through my teeth at the pain in my chest, making it difficult to draw in a proper breath. I'm literally going to have a bruise shaped as a boot print. My chin drops to my chest with my shoulders curving to appear smaller.

"I'm sorry." My voice comes out choked, desperation clear in my tone as I sit there shaking.

"You will be. Tell me, what do you think of Cruz? Do you fancy him?" He asks absently, leaning over the table to his right as he snorts coke in a straight line, he shakes his head as he sinks back into the chair.

He's gazing across the room and when I follow his gaze, Cruz is leaning against the bar with my mom stroking his cock over his jeans as he stares at me without blinking.

I'm at a loss for words. I feel like this is a test. Did Cruz really talk to him earlier or was he only messing with me to stalk me like the creep he is?

"I think- I'm not. What does-," I'm cut off as Payne bursts into laughter that causes everyone else to laugh and the music to start playing again.

"So pathetic. Get out of my sight girl." He waves his hand dismissing me as he starts kissing Doris' neck but her attention is right on me.

Her eyes are still wide and I see the fear in them but not for her. For me. She gives a small jerk of her chin, telling me to get out of here. To get away from the man whose mission in life is to cause me unbearable pain until I'm all cut up and it's damn hard to escape at that point. Cruz can't have me and he knows it unless Payne gives him a signal that I'm free game so he's resorted to Lorrie instead. She makes me sick especially when she drops down to her knees in front of Cruz and unbuckles his belt, which gives me flashbacks at night of him taking it off with the metal hooks clinking together. Funny how the smallest thing can control us, like a noise or smell that brings it all back in seconds.

I don't waste time to get away, I'm halfway across the room in seconds and ignoring the hands groping my breasts and squeezing my ass when I pass by with my head down. It doesn't matter because I can't see their faces, too many club members crowded in one place. It could be all of them or none at all, just phantom hands from my past that I can't escape. I'm losing my mind.

That's me, Tillie, the girl who can't fight back and I begin to wonder if this is how it all ends. There is no fork in the road for me, it's just a straight road into misery. Collapsing onto my bed after shoving my desk chair under my doorknob, I stare up at my ceiling fan as it slowly spins.

Am I tired? Yes, but the moment I close my eyes, my brain shuts off and the nightmares happen that cause me to wake up screaming into my pillow as I bite it to stifle the almost inhuman sounds I make. To top my night off... I still have homework to do and school in a couple of hours.

CHAPTER 3

Tillie

*B*reath in... breath out...

The scent alone causes me to cower, to breathe from my mouth so I can pretend he's not in the room with me. The windowless basement with the smell of mold and the tangy taste of copper lingering in the air is something I'll never be able to erase from my senses. Welcome to the darkest, deepest part of my memory. Fuck you memories, you think I want to repeat this in my head a thousand times a day? No, but the brain is a fickle thing because it doesn't listen to you one bit, you're basically a puppet being pulled by the puppet master.

"Have you learned your lesson yet, Daughter?" Payne's voice echoes off the walls but I can't pinpoint his hiding spot in the shadows.

It's only been two weeks since my fallen disgrace happened in here and yet here I am again. Strung up to the rafters, the cuffs digging into my shredded wrists, and the floor above my head soaking in my wails.

"Yes." My voice is so quiet a mouse wouldn't be able to hear me.

Did I sit in my bedroom, stiff in the corner of the room with my arms wrapped around myself like a barrier for a week straight? Yes, and I knew he'd come for me eventually, his timing perfect because the bruises had just started to fade to yellow and brown. A fresh area to mark me again.

"What's that, girl? Speak up!" He appears in front of me like the grim reaper coming from the dark, his voice booming in my face and hooking his fist into my solar plexus without warning.

I imagine this is what it feels like to have someone bring you back from the dead, a whooshing breath of that first inhale and trying to escape the memory of dying.

"Yes!" My hoarse voice shouts, my head falling on my shoulder from being too weak to hold myself up.

"That's good, very good. Now the real fun can begin in your training. Unless you'd rather have a repeat of having cocks shoved inside your cunt again until you learn to shut up?" His brown eyes gleam, almost anticipating my answer, the sick bastard.

If I had the strength, I'd kill him myself while shoving Cruz's boots up his ass until it comes out of his mouth and gutting Cruz like a fish at the same time. A thousand stabs of death until my darkest memories are gone. My thoughts are dark and scary, not mine anymore because this Tillie has seen the evil in the real world and her eyes are wide open now despite not wanting to be welcomed with open arms by the devil. The man who is supposed to love me with his whole heart waits for my answer and my words are caught in my throat so I can only nod. I guess his heart was ripped out as a young child when he was innocent and fed to the wolves with sharp teeth that gleamed with blood. Innocence has to disappear at some point whether we want it to or not.

"That's what I thought. It's time, little Tillie." He walks over to the wall where a pegboard of torture devices hang, the sight of it twists my stomach in knots. Payne swipes his toy off the hook, turning back to me with a malicious smile.

No!

His boots scrape over the floor towards me, the sound louder than it should be.

"Tillie." My voice is being called softly but his lips aren't moving. He pulls the whip up to my face so I can see what will make me bleed and I'm already screaming before it can even touch my back as he moves behind me.

"Tillie," whispers a soft voice again, causing my dream to blur around the edges, the image shattering like a broken glass of milk falling from the counter until it's a running mess with sharpened points.

I sit up in my bed gasping, the tangled sheets under me drenched from my tears and sweat coating my shaking body.

My whole body gives one big shiver, trying to shake off the dream that likes to mess with my mind. I run a trembling hand through my hair to push the sweat soaked stains out of my eyes while reaching for my phone to see that it's five in the morning and I have about an hour before the alarm goes off for school. There's no way I can fall back asleep after that dream, might as well start getting ready for the day. My foot touches the floor just as a small scraping sound comes from my bedroom door. My eyes fly over to see the chair still tucked underneath and it's a little easier to breathe after seeing that it held sturdy.

"Tillie, open up. Hurry," whispers a familiar faint female voice on the other side of the door.

The compound is still dark along with the sky that is just starting to turn a greyish/blue, a hint that the sunrise is coming. Everyone should still be passed out somewhere with hangovers and their dicks exposed to the cold morning air. Sliding out of bed the rest of the way on quiet feet, I pad over to the door and place my ear against the weakened wood to hear soft breathing on the other side.

"It's me, Doris." I'm already picking up the chair before she finishes that sentence and cracking open the door to see her panicked face on the other side.

She pushes through the door, shoving me out of the way and quietly shutting it behind her with a wince. If it was anyone else, I'd be running for my window to find a way out but Doris has been like the mother I've never had. Looking out for me when she could, just overall protecting me the best way a person in her position can. She's stuck in this place too, realizing a long time ago that once in the club, there is no other place you will belong.

"What is going on? Doris, what are you doing!" I hiss under my breath, freaking the fuck out as she rushes around my room with a duffle bag collecting my stuff with trembling hands.

She just continues to pack, opening my drawers, not saying a thing. Having enough, I place my hands on her shoulders to spin her around to face me. Her brown eyes are blown wide with fear, filling with tears as she looks at my face before pulling me into a tight hug.

My arms hang loose at my sides, knowing that whatever she's doing... She's saying goodbye because Doris doesn't hug.

"It's time to fly free, girl," she whispers into my hair and shoves the duffle bag and my helmet into my numb hands along with my leather jacket.

"What are you talking about?" To my own ears, my voice comes out hollow and broken because she gives me this false hope that there is a place for me besides here.

I'm fucking terrified.

"You need to run. Should have been running five minutes ago, years ago." She wipes sweat from her forehead, looking like she's aged ten years with wrinkles more pronounced around her tight lipped mouth. "He's going to give you away, Tillie. I need to get you out of here, and I finally found her after looking for so long." Her rambling words don't make sense as she quietly opens my bedroom door, looking both ways.

She reaches back and grabs my hand, dragging me along with her down the dark hallway lined with closed bedroom doors as my body follows like I'm really not there. She pauses at the staircase, peaking around the corner, straining to see if anyone is moving below. With a yank, she pulls me down the stairs after her and makes her way towards the back kitchen door, stepping over a passed out Joker. I swear she's barely breathing. I know to keep quiet so I don't say a word until we're outside with the door shutting softly behind us.

"Give me away? What is happening right now?" My lungs hurt, and feel like my heart is going to explode out my chest and paint the compound red.

We round the corner to my bike and she takes the duffle bag from my fingers to strap on the back of the bike while her eyes dart around, looking for any movement.

"Cruz. Payne's going to give you to Cruz. You'd be his old

lady, Tillie, and I know in my heart you wouldn't make it to next year." The blood drains from my face as I sway on my feet, she steadies me by gripping my forearms so I'm focused on her face. "You're going to do exactly as I say, okay?" She searches my face before nodding, making sure everything she's saying is absorbing through my shock.

"Get on your bike, drive far enough into the desert until it's undecided which way you could have gone and crash it, okay? Then, you need to hitch a ride to downtown Las Vegas, your trail can get lost there to buy you time. Get on a greyhound bus for a ticket to New York but pay with cash and tell the clerk that you're running from an abusive husband, they should keep that on the down low, hopefully. You really need a ticket for Los Angeles instead, you need to disappear. I want you to hide your face from any and all cameras, and dye your hair with the color I put in the bag once you get off your stop. Make sure your hoodie is pulled up." She helps me put my helmet on because my hands are shaking too hard, this is happening too fast.

I'm not ready.

"Can't you come with me-"

She's already shaking her head and pulls me into another hug which I return this time because this is really goodbye. "No, I have to appear normal and hide you no matter what. Tillie, remember this address and repeat it over and over until it sticks. She's the only safe place and I hope one day you'll forgive me for not telling you. I have to make sure they can't find you, it's all I have left to give and I should have done this years ago." She places a piece of paper in my hand and pulls down my visor, nodding towards the gates.

"Who-" My words are cut off once again, but this time at

the sound of the rusty chained gate dragging open and Doris is gone by the time I look over, no doubt crawling back into Payne's bed before he notices she was ever gone.

Not wasting another second, my bike roars to life, making me wince as I kick the stand up and rush through the now closing gate with a prospect turning a blind eye and locking the gates back up. Not everyone in the club is bad but it's only a small handful to a full army. My heart races along with my engine the farther I make it away from the compound. It's either crawl on my knees behind Cruz for the rest of my short miserable life or fly fucking free.

It's simple, live or die.

I'm going to live but where the hell is Doris sending me?

I know a curve is coming up on the deserted road ahead of me just outside of the Mojave Desert and it's the perfect spot to crash my bike. It's far enough away from the Demon Jokers and plenty of time to mislead them because once they find out I'm gone... a manhunt will begin. Cruz will never let me go free unless it's on the river of the dead. It's only a matter of time until he finds me, the Demon Jokers have eyes and ears everywhere. This will at least buy me some time.

The hot desert sun is already beating on my back in waves, the wind just as restricting and it's only been an hour since I left the compound. They're probably already getting up and doing the usual club business shit. My time is running out and I can't stop clenching the handlebars because it's hard to let go of something that actually had a good memory for me. My bike starts to lean with the curve straight ahead and I twist the throttle one last time for a bit of speed before releasing the gas.

This is going to hurt.

My hands slowly release the handlebars on the curve going just a little over thirty, my bike gliding with the road and it almost feels like I'm flying with my arms stretched out over my head just for a second. I reach back quickly and unstrap my duffle bag with one hand, hugging it to my chest just as the bike wobbles under me. My crotch rocket starts tipping to the side, my body moves with it until I'm pushing my feet off footrests and falling onto the asphalt with the bike crashing to the ground, skidding along the road, causing sparks to fly. I keep sliding along the road on my side in a momentum that makes me feel breathless, my body rolling and bouncing off the burning hot road with rocks digging into my back. My leather jacket and helmet offer some protection but my jacket is ripped to shreds and my helmet scratched to hell by the time I come to a stop.

I lay there, trying to catch my breath and take in the injuries to my body. My leg is burning and something hot drips down the side of my calf but other than that, I'm just real fucking dizzy. Sitting up with a grimace, I take my helmet off with a head shake and pant with each breath. I slide off my jacket mournfully and chuck it into the desert with my anger. Sitting there in the freaking middle of the road in the middle of nowhere, I pluck at my ripped skinny jeans without looking at my throbbing leg, feeling pity for myself. It takes me a minute but I eventually gather the courage to look over at my bike.

A whimper escapes my mouth as soon as I see my bike broken on the side of the road, pieces literally scattered across the ground. It's a heap of metal, unrecognizable beside the stripes of purple that glint off the steel chrome.

The Demon Jokers will be able to tell it's mine once it's called in. A motorcycle crash will make it back to the club even this far out. They stick to their own kind and news travels fast. The Demon Jokers practically run Las Vegas.

I'm really feeling that dull ache in my leg the moment I stand and it takes a lot not to look down as I start limping away from the wreckage in the opposite direction. The helmet means nothing to me now, tossing it into the pile of broken pieces seemed like a good idea.

I've been walking for what seems like an hour, sweat gathers at my hairline and the sun is blaring down on me at this point that it's hard to tell in the distance if a car is heading my way or if it's a fragment of my imagination. I'm praying it's a car that is willing to take a passenger. Almost scared to look, debating if I should make a run for it in the desert because what if it's Cruz? He would drag me back kicking and screaming from the underworld just to torture me himself.

I can't help it, my body angles off the road onto the dry dirt but a rush of air expands from my lungs when I see it's just a truck driver. Sticking my thumb out, I walk backwards and try to appear normal. As if I'd know what that looks like. The trucker honks his horn, it's a guy which I can tell by the low ball cap and beard from my lower position from the ground, and he starts to slow down near me on the side of the road. Yeah, probably not the best idea to hitchhike with a stranger but what are my options? Besides this guy is probably a freaking daisy amongst a field of poison ivy. He leans over and opens the door with a friendly smile, warm brown eyes with crow's feet at the corner.

"Hey, little lady, need a ride? Always wanted to say that." He chuckles at his own little joke as I hide an eye roll before stepping up into the truck with a small jump and grabbing the oh shit bar to heave myself up onto the seat.

He isn't a bad looking guy, pretty young for living on the road. A nice smile, friendly brown eyes that don't frighten me, and doesn't have an overbearing air about him. If I was a normal girl, I'd probably want to date a guy like him if I was looking for a normal, boring future. A family man, simple life. Too bad that's not for someone like me.

Hiding a wince from the pain in my leg, I shuffle in the big seat until I'm somewhat comfortable. He waits for my answer, not even putting the truck into gear.

"Um yeah. You wouldn't be heading to Las Vegas near the strip by chance?" I have to clear my throat a few times so my voice sounds not so scratchy from walking in the middle of the desert for God knows how long.

"Sure am! Want a water?" He asks, but is already leaning back for a bottle of water, his face is suddenly very close to my boobs as he tries to reach behind his seat.

He seems to notice this at the same time when he pauses and stares before shaking his head. He quickly sits back up in his seat, handing me the water and blushing a bright red.

Hmm... maybe this trucker isn't one of the bad ones. He's kind of cute in a lumberjack way even with the slight dad bod he has going on and the beard probably covering a baby face but it works for him.

"Thanks." I turn away from him, his staring making me uncomfortable as if he's looking for something in my gaze. I twist the cap off to chug the water with a moan because it feels so good going down my dry throat.

He clears his throat and starts the semi, finally heading south on the open road towards the city of sin. It's funny, I think sin shouldn't be defined in one place because everyone is a sinner in one form or another. I guess more are drawn to a city that is made for sinning and gives you an excuse to be bad where the secrets stay. Too bad that's my life definition everyday.

"So, why Las Vegas? Did you have some car trouble, that's why you were on the side of the road?" He's already nodding his head like that explains it and I'll let him keep thinking that, guess we were doing the small talk.

I prop my elbow on the windowsill and stare outside to see the desert, that all looks the same, pass by in a blur.

"Yup, car trouble. Can you drop me off on south main street at the Greyhound bus station?" I try to keep my tone neutral and bored so he doesn't suspect anything because who wouldn't when a girl is walking alone on the deserted road?

I mean come on, my pants are ripped up at the knees with a bloodstain on my calf and my white tank top is sticking to my skin from sweating. I'm not exactly the most put together right now.

"Where are you heading from there?" He asks slowly and I turn to look at him staring at the road with furrowed brows as if he's starting to finally question why I'm out in the middle of nowhere.

"Visiting family." My lame excuse rushes out to make him believe that something like that is as simple as it sounds, which works when his expression clears so I try to direct the conversation somewhere else before he asks more unwanted questions. "How long have you been on the road?"

He sits up straighter and flashes me a smile before tapping the bobblehead of a woman in a Hawaiian skirt. He couldn't be any more normal and boring if he tried.

"Me and my girl here have been on the road for a couple of years after getting out of school. It's the easy life, ya know?

43

Just me and the open road. I always wanted to travel the world and this comes pretty close to it." He winks and takes his ball cap off to nervously scratch his brown hair that's surprisingly not receding before placing it back on top of his head. "Gets kind of lonely though but we sign up for this stuff all on our own." His expression falls and damn if I don't feel bad for him.

I completely understand being lonely even when you're in a crowded room, all you have is you and yourself. The only difference is this guy chose to get in this truck and live his life to the happiest he can... me not so much. Choices get taken away. It's in that moment when I notice that I have a choice right the fuck now. I'm out in the open, not under Payne's thumb with watchful eyes. I may be on the run but it's my decision. I'm just going to have to be careful to not end up back in that monster's fingertips.

"Totally. Hey, what's your name?" I'm going to remember this trucker who helped give me an escape even if he didn't know it. He's really one of the good ones out there.

"Adam. What about you, little lady?" He draws out with a chuckle, tipping his hat at me in a cheesy manner.

This I have to be careful with because I haven't decided what to do about my name. It's a way to come up with something new but it's just easier to go by Tillie. I'll just have to give a different last name.

"Tillie Jones. Nice to meet ya, trucker Adam." I offer a hesitant smile which only causes him to practically beam at me and stick out his hand for me to shake.

I eye his hand like it might somehow bite me and decide this guy can't possibly hurt me more than I already have been. My hand clasps his with a small shake before I quickly let go and fiddle with the radio to offer a distraction because that small touch is freaking me out. A simple, common touch shouldn't scare people but it does for me. I'll never be normal. The rest of the ride is quiet except for the random questions he asks with the radio softly playing in the background. My shoulders gradually relax somewhat but it's only the beginning of my journey and I'm automatically taught to trust no one.

CHAPTER 4

Cruz

"You fucking find her. I want all of you fucking cunts out there looking for her! Ears and eyes, am I fucking clear?" Payne shouts angrily, dismissing Church as he slams his fist on the table when he gets mumbled affirmatives in return.

Everyone scatters out of the room with their tails tucked between their legs but I stay behind, propping my feet up on the ledge of the table, my hands clasped together behind my head. I can handle Payne's violent outbursts of anger because my own is nothing compared to his... it's worse. I feel absolutely nothing inside, it's a fucking dark, empty echo, and my obsession is the one girl who doesn't want me. I thought claiming that cunt would keep her in her place, but she just had to get out of line and run off. But, no worries. I love a good hunt and she's at the top of my list. I can hardly wait to break her in once I find her.

"Cruz, I want you to go find her, and if you return with

her... She's yours, boy. I don't fucking care if you slit her throat while fucking her. Tillie will learn who is in command right under my boot for one last time. But first, I need you to do something for me."

I tilt my head, staring at him, and wonder why I don't feel an ounce of compassion for his daughter. Being abandoned at a young age by their birth parents would screw anyone up in the head but that's the thing, I was already messed up since birth. Growing up, I once saw an animal and had a desire to cut it up just to see how its insides worked. The words sociopath repeated from multiple doctors still lingers, the main reason my parents left me at the park and never returned, but Payne took one look at me and gazed past the chemically imbalanced part of my brain. He gave me a home where I could run the city red and didn't blink once, especially when I became obsessed with his daughter. I've waited patiently, followed his orders, fucked his daughter when he allowed it and I'm finally close to taking what's been mine from day one. Tillie will be mine even if I have to kill her and claim the last bit of light leaving her eyes, I'll even have her soul because she can't escape me. So, I'll fucking do anything and it's finally my time to shine.

"What do you need from me?" I nick my finger with my knife, watching the trail of red liquid slide out of the cut, and can picture clear as day when I carved up Tillie's back with my initials, her blood running freely onto my hands.

"I have a rat and I need you to sniff them out. You'll find the girl faster. It's only a matter of time." Payne grins slowly, stroking his beard as he stares out the window overlooking the junkyard. "No one runs from me, no one."

CHAPTER 5

Tillie

"Well here we are, um... be careful out there," Adam says, taking his cap off again nervously and glancing at my breasts as if he can't help himself, his throat bobbing as he turns off the semi in the bus stop parking lot.

God, this poor guy. I may not have much to give but I have something most girls don't. The key to seduction and knowing how to use my body.

"Adam, get in the back cab," I tell him in a low voice, watching his eyes snap up to mine in confusion.

"W-what?" He stutters out and I can already see the tent growing in his pants, it's easier to do this after seeing he's not packing a monster in those jeans.

"This is my thank you." He shakes his head, about to say no until I grab the hem of my tank top and throw it on the dashboard in one swoop.

He freezes in his seat, eyes widening as he stares at my

breasts again like they are the answer to the universe. Men are all the same, give them a little love and they're putty in your hands.

"Adam..." His eyes meet mine. "Back. Seat. Now." My voice comes out husky to get him moving and I'm about to lose my nerve when he quickly unbuckles his seatbelt, cursing when it gets tangled in his arm before dodging into the back between the seats.

With a deep breath, I give myself a pep talk

You control your body. This is your decision. Give this guy a memory for his lonely nights on the road because he's helped you when most wouldn't.

My body moves without really thinking too much about it, and before I know it, I'm climbing onto this trucker's lap who is already panting. This isn't going to take long and I'm a damn good professional at giving lap dances. I've been in this seat plenty of times even when I didn't want to. Doris taught me all I needed to know to drive a man crazy with lust and how fast it takes to get him off. God that's so pathetic, what an accomplishment I've achieved in life. Go me, giving lap dances like a champ. Adam starts to raise his hands to place on my body but I stop him before he can touch me.

"I'm going to rock your world, give you a memory to look back on when you're feeling lonely, and for helping a girl on the side of the road without asking for anything in return. Just don't touch me and I'll do all the work okay?"

He looks like he's about to interject but my hands are unclasping my bra in the front as my legs squeeze the outside of his thighs from my straddle position. His attention focuses on my naked breasts and his breath fans my collarbone as his hands drop down to his sides limply. I look behind his shoulder at the wall as I plant my ass on his denim covered dick, grinding down against him.

"Sweet Jesus," he mutters in a daze when my hips roll over him again and again, rubbing against his dick in the right way that will have him blowing his load in seconds.

He needs to come now because my vision is getting grey around the edges, putting me in a place I'd rather not be.

Take it slut. God, look at her loving my dick, can't get enough of her cunt being filled with my jizz. Say please, Tillie, and tell us that you want to get fucked by all of us.

Not now.

Every single time I've had to do this, climbing onto a stranger's lap just so they can experience pleasure from my body that doesn't want to do this, that night always resurfaces like a wave crashing on the sand, it just keeps coming back. I can feel their phantom hands on my body as they defile me over and over again.

My body moves on autopilot, growing wet between my legs as I rub my clothed pussy right over his dick despite not really feeling anything inside. It's like instinct to feel what the body craves but can't have because our minds fuck us up in the end. Needing this to be over, I drag my heated core right over him just as I lean back, my back arched until I'm staring at the grey fabric of the truck ceiling. I play with my nipples in front of his face to give him the perfect view. He'll be done soon. Would it be wrong of me if I started laughing when I feel him spasming under me and hearing him let out a whimper as he came? It's almost unfair how I can't do that, just let go and feel something that makes you cry out in pleasure inside instead of screaming in pain.

I'm off of his lap before he's even finished and skip my bra altogether as I shove my tank top over my head while he sits there in a daze. I unzip my bag and grab a hoodie to cover my body with the hood hiding my face from any cameras in the parking lot. The walls start closing in on me as I reach for the handle to get out of the truck. My world is focusing back into color but tortuous memories creep along the edges of my mind.

"Wait! Who are you, Tillie Jones?" He pants out in a desperate tone.

"I'm the devil's spawn baby and it's best for you to try to forget my face because it could lead you to trouble one day." A small warning for him because if anyone finds out he helped me... I can't think that way right now.

"As if I'd forget you," he whispers with a small laugh of disbelief.

I glance over my shoulder at him, smiling like I have a secret, taking in his pink cheeks under his beard along with his disheveled hair and the wet stain on his jeans before hopping down from the passenger door.

"I didn't say forget me, you can remember my body for the lonely nights on the road. Bye, Trucker Adam." I wink at him and take off running towards the bus station before he can say anything else.

I controlled that moment in the back of the cab... my decision and my fucking body to do as it pleases.

It's an awakening that sparks something deep inside of me that I'm scared to look too closely at. It's still scary as hell because what limits does my own body have when I decide that I'm taking the reins?

The sliding glass doors of the bus station offer a blast of cold air on my heated skin, clearing my head as I scan the lobby for anyone dressed in a leather cut. I mean it's not just leather I have to be on the lookout for because their sources extend farther than just the club. You have the buyers that pay a pretty penny for the best drugs, the other clubs that are known in other countries, or the worst you really have to look for is the people that fear them. People do crazy things when their heart races from the unknown and that could be my downfall for being caught. Luckily it's pretty empty, the blue and white checkered floors are spotless which tells me not much traffic comes through here. The clerk and the one sleeping homeless man on the bench are the only people I see. Most people travel by plane or car these days, no one wants to sit next to a stranger for countless hours on a bus.

I approach the counter, my head down and my hood covering my face from the camera in the corner of the room behind the clerk who hasn't bothered to look up from her slouched position in her chair with her feet kicked up on the counter. She blows a piece of pink bubble gum, snapping the bubble when she finally lazily looks up at me with a bored expression on her face.

"Um, one ticket to New York, one way, please." My voice comes out as a hushed whisper.

She pops another bubble, the noise making me cringe in the quiet space. Rolling her eyes, she plops her feet down as she enters the information into her computer to print me a ticket. The piercing on her face reflects off the low lighting as she glances back at me with a raised brow as my ticket slowly prints before sliding it across on the counter towards me. I dig money out of my bag and hand it over without a word. She's about to pick up her cell phone, going back to ignoring me but I clear my throat which only has her sighing in annoyance.

"Yeah, anything else?" She drawls with another loud bubble pop.

"One way ticket to Los Angeles too." My hand shakes as I start to hand her more money because this chick is staring at me with a curious expression now.

"You sure about that?" She questions, looking me up and down before her gaze stops on the bloodstain seeping through my pants from the bike crash.

She looks like she's about to call the cops or something by the way she keeps looking at me and my disheveled appearance then back to her phone. Shit. I can't have that because I'm pretty sure the cops around here are in Payne's pockets.

"Listen, I need to disappear," I tell her quickly, thinking of what Doris told me, about saying I'm running from a husband but I don't think she'll believe me. "I'm trying to get away from an abusive ex before it's too late for me." I'm really not lying too much because Cruz is an ex who deserves to die so I think I'm selling this to her.

She sits up straight, quickly prints my new ticket, and slips my cash back to me.

"Keep it, and you're doing the right thing. Us girls have to look out for each other, fuck those fuck boys. Girl power." She holds her fist out for me to bump which I do hesitantly and I'm betting this chick goes to all the women's rights marches.

"Thanks." She nods once and I plaster on a fake smile before turning around to get the heck out of there, really hoping she doesn't think calling the police is the best option.

Once again, the Nevada heat absorbs into my skin the moment I step outside to find my bus. My ticket says it is departing at one, that's in thirty minutes. It's a little nerve wracking because I have a feeling Payne and Cruz are going to be tearing this city apart very soon looking for me. That's what someone who owns an object does, you don't stop looking until it's found.

Finding bus number twenty-nine, I quicken my pace and

climb the stairs with my hair covering my face, the bus driver barely glancing at me. Empty seats except for three are occupied which is a blessing. The fewer people that see me, the less likely I'll be remembered. Taking a seat at the back of the bus, I fall against the cushioned fabric, a slow drawn out sigh escaping me. I've made it this far, only a little more to go. Reaching into my jeans' pocket, I gaze at the address, blinking with disbelief at fourteen ninety Monica Beverly Hills, California. Who the hell is this person Doris is sending me to? The land of the rich and privileged, how does she know anyone that would live there? Am I doing the right thing? If Cruz finds me, I don't think I'll ever see the light of day again and Tillie will just be a name someone forgets about after she disappears into the ring of human trafficking or six feet under ground.

Please God let this be the right choice because if not, I'm as good as dead.

At least the purple dye in my hair isn't a big dramatic change, I mean it stands out pretty well as I turn my head side to side in the mirror after I dried it under the bathroom hand dryer. It kind of blends in with my long dark hair, never trust a box of hair dye. At least I made it in one piece even if the whole time I was a mess at each bus stop with people coming and going. Two days flew by on the bus and I'm finally in Los Angeles, I can hardly believe it... I've never even been outside of Nevada. I'm beyond tired, exhausted to a new level, and feeling kind of gross being stuck in a tin can for hours. The dye was a cheap one and it's making my scalp itch but at least it does the job at making me look somewhat different. Bracing my hands against the sink, I take a deep breath before heading out into the unknown. Pushing past the automatic doors, I stand on the curb waiting for a taxi to pass and hope no one asks any questions about why a girl is traveling in the middle of the night by herself. Just as my luck would have it, rain starts to pour down like the floodgates opened and I'm soaked in seconds. So much for drying my hair, the top of my shirt is now stained a light purple as the dye continues to wash off.

Squinting, I wave down a taxi just as it turns the corner before halting in front of me. I get into the cab, and give the taxi driver the address, before I know it I'm heading right towards a stranger's house that's supposed to help me. City lights pass by in a blur, people walking in groups as they enter a club or restaurant while laughing in a carefree way and I can't help but wonder what that feels like. Palm trees line on either side of the streets and rolling down the window, you can practically taste the salt from the ocean in the air. It's a busy city and the closer I get to Beverly Hills, the rich start to come out of the woodwork with their flashy sports cars, and people wearing designer brands like it's attached to their bodies at birth. My own clothes scream outcast, sticking out like a sore thumb with too short shorts that shape to my butt like a warm hug and a light sweater that's stained and a little bit see through with the mesh material, a sliver of my stomach showing, and my tattoos on display. Black combat boots complete my look. You may escape the biker atmosphere but you can't take the biker out of the girl. Doesn't help that my clothes are sticking to my body from the rain and my hair is wet, with water dripping down my back, making me shiver in the back seat. I'm anxious to get out of the cab, I catch the driver glancing back every few seconds, his mirror angled towards my breasts.

Sometimes I really hate men. I just want to be that bad bitch who takes what she wants, when she wants it, instead of living in fear that someone will take it without permission. He starts to slow down with his blinker on as he pulls onto a street lined with mansions that have long, curving driveways on hills that end at the road with gates to keep the riff-raff out.

I can already tell I don't belong here. What am I doing?

The driver comes to a stop at a dead end with the last house on the street, a winding private driveway leading to a mansion that sits on a hill. An iron gate with a capital R branded on the front blocks most of the view and rows of tall palm trees on either side.

"You sure this is the right address?" He asks skeptically, dragging his gaze over my drowned self, flashing his eyes back towards the mansion.

I have no fucking clue if this is where I'm actually supposed to be but it's written in Doris' handwriting and I don't think she'd send me somewhere that I could be found. I hope.

"Yea, thanks. Keep the change." I'm already halfway up the driveway when the taxi drives away, muttering to himself with his window down so I hear half of what he's complaining about.

Something about rich fuckers? Yeah buddy, I completely agree.

I'm shaking with nerves every step of the way until I stop at the gate next to an intercom. Pushing the button after a deep exhale, I stand there for a while with a light drizzle falling from the sky now and wondering if anyone's actually home. I'm about to give up and find a way to get back into the city to stay at a cheap hotel when a voice travels through the speakers.

"Yes?" The soft voice scares the crap out of me, making my heart pound as I push the button again.

"Hi, um, I'm a friend of Doris and she sent me here. I think I'm at the right place..." I trail off, my hands shaking and I start to feel the panic set in.

I wait for her to reply and it goes so quiet that I can hear my own breathing, making me think I got the wrong place until the gates smoothly start to swing open. Gripping my duffle bag, I climb up the long driveway that feels like I've been walking for hours but is probably only a few minutes until I'm standing in front of a set of huge double doors. There are floor to ceiling glass windows on either side of a mahogany door. Looking around, I figured the woman would meet me at the door since she let me through the gates. My knuckles tap softly on the glass and I can see a shadow move on the other side of the windows.

Okay then... maybe I should come back?

The door swings open in a rush, a woman in her early forties stands there with wide brown eyes as she takes in my appearance on her expensive doormat.

"Who are you?" She asks in a shaky voice, not looking away from my face like she's staring at a ghost as her trembling hand clutches the pearls around her neck.

There is something oddly familiar about her. I stare at her like I know her, trying to place where from. Brown eyes stare back at me, her skin bronzed naturally from the side of her that looks Latina. She's slightly shorter than me and her hair dyed a fake blonde, not matching her dark eyebrows.

Where the hell do I know her from?!

"My name is Tillie, a friend of mine, Doris sent m-" She drops like a sack of potatoes at my boots, a small scream leaving her mouth, and her eyes rolling to the back of her head.

I stand there frozen for a second, not sure what just happened before dropping my bag and crouching at her side to check her pulse. Is she on drugs? I've seen this before plenty of times as a bad case of coke slipped into the club unnoticed. Payne had prospects test that stuff out before passing it around to the members and selling it to their buyers. Did the rich really need drugs to escape from a life where they have everything they could possibly want?

Silly drugs, messes up lives everywhere in seconds. Doesn't matter if you're poor or rich I guess.

A sturdy thump under my fingertips tells me she's at least alive so that's good and her eyelids are fluttering as she starts to come around.

"Who the hell are you?" Startled, I glance up quickly from my crouched position to see a man walking calmly down a long hallway towards us, the heels of his shoes clicking over the marble floor. "What have you done to her?!" He snaps, his face stoic but I can see the controlled rage burning in his gaze as he finally reaches my side.

The air around him is suffocating, almost unbearable. I can recognize a man of power and this man has it in waves. He's dressed in an expensive suit, a Rolex gleaming on his wrist as he slicks back his greying hair at his temples but the look he gives me stops my breathing. He has the look of a cop with that hard stare, but no way a man on a cop salary would dress like that. His hazel eyes narrow at me with suspicion the longer I stare. I feel like I'm under a spotlight with the hard glint his eyes are giving me. What the fuck? The fainting lady is the one that let me through the gate, glare at her instead!

"I didn't do anything! She fainted, I swear." I gesture towards the lady at my feet, my palms out as I stand up and back away so he can check her over as he glares at me some more. "I'm Tillie."

"Tillie," the lady mutters, her eyes snapping open with a gasp as if she's drowning, and looks up at me with tears gathering in her eyes.

"Uh, yeah, that's me. Look, I don't want any trouble so I'll just be going now. Sorry for bothering you." My palms sweat and my boots shuffle backwards on the floor, probably leaving black scuff marks but I need to get away from them.

As if he could read my thoughts, he snatches my wrist in a hard grip and points inside his house, practically dragging me into the hallway.

"Inside, now! You're not going anywhere until I get some answers," he says in such an authoritative voice that I'm already moving through their entryway before I know it.

Damn, he's scary. I mean I've dealt with worse but I'm not turning my back on this guy. He lets go of my wrist once he gets me inside the house, more like trapped so he can keep me in his line of sight. He helps- who I'm assuming is his wife- off the floor, placing an arm around her waist as he walks her into their huge living room with me trailing after them at a safe distance. This guy practically screams wealth and power, down to his Italian loafers and his slicked back salt and pepper hair. I swear this guy even walks like an officer, never taking his gaze off me. I've known what to look for, having to when you grow up in a compound of murderers and thieves, but what puzzles me is how this guy can afford a house like this on a police salary. Maybe his wife is the rich one? My internal thoughts come to a stop when I realize they are both staring at me, waiting to speak from their position on the large sectional white couch that takes up half the room. I'm almost scared to touch anything. I've never seen a floor so clean that my reflection shows off the surface, I'm used to floors with blood stained into the wood and body fluids I'd rather not think about.

"So yeah, Doris sent me to this address. Do you know her?" I ask the fainting wifey warily and there she goes again holding her pearls.

"Sweetbutt," she whispers under her breath in a daze and blinks rapidly at my slow nod.

What is wrong with this lady?

"H-how old are you?" She stumbles over her words like she's drunk, maybe she is and I'm wrong about the drugs.

"Just turned eighteen yesterday," I tell her, eyeing her for any crazy movements like she might go psycho on my ass and pull a gun.

It takes me a second to realize that I am now an adult, it feels like a lifetime has passed when in reality it's only been a few days since I left the compound.

Forgetting one's birthday is a normal thing unless you had an Uncle Rig in your life who treasured each one like you'd die tomorrow. I forgot it was my birthday yesterday and what a way to celebrate, I mean I guess freedom isn't the worst thing for a gift. Could be the reason Payne decided to gift *me* to Cruz.

She starts hyperventilating, clenching her husband's hand, and starts to sway on the couch.

"Look at her eyes, Franco, look. It's my Till." She passes out again on the spot across her husband's lap but he hardly notices because he's staring me down with suspicion that hasn't stopped since I stepped into the house.

He's looking at me like I'm a bug beneath his shoe or he's about to whip out a forty caliber glock on me and send me swimming with the fishes. The whiplash between cop and godfather is giving me a headache. Does he not notice his wife passed out on his lap? I bet he's wondering what the hell I'm doing here.

I can't believe it either buddy because I have no clue what's going on and why she called me her Till like Uncle Rig used to do. Ted seems to shake himself and scoops his wife up into his arms as he stands but stops to look down at me.

"I'm going to lay her down. This is a shock for her and I think it would be best if you stay here until she's feeling better because I'm sure you both want some answers. Make yourself at home but don't fucking steal anything," he warns and I can hear more of the threat under his words, telling me that he has his eye on me if I try anything.

He strides out of the room with his shoes tapping on the marble floor until I can't hear him anymore once he disappears somewhere in the maze of their over the top large mansion. I scoff under my breath.

As if I'd steal from this house, I wouldn't make it past the front door. Everything looks heavy as hell and breakable. Being left alone gives me a chance to really look around because everything just happened too fast to really take in my surroundings. Spinning in a circle, the living room is floor to ceiling windows that overlook the valley and city lights in the distance. It's unbelievable, breathtaking, and kind of freaks me out. I've never been in a place like this. Ted did say to make myself at home which is weird to tell a complete stranger, but whatever. I have an itch to explore and by how my stomach is rumbling, it's leading me right towards the kitchen before I know what I'm doing. When was the last time I ate? Two days ago? My boots are probably leaving scuff marks on the floor from dragging my feet and a trail of puddles since I'm still wet from the rain and shaking from the cold. I walk down a long hallway with dim lighting, the walls displaying framed art probably worth more than this house. My boots keep squeaking, like a wet squishy sound and it reminds me of when just a few days ago I was sneaking around the compound on my tippy toes just so no one comes to investigate the noises. I've been walking on my toes for such a long time that I've grown used to the silence, so I kick off my shoes along with my gross wet socks, placing them at the entrance of the kitchen.

Oh. My. God.

Is this a kitchen? It's too damn big and everything gleams that it almost hurts my eyes. I swear the kitchen island could sleep ten people on top of the rose quartz counter. Making my way towards the industrial fridge, I pull the door open, and my mouth waters at all the food inside. I'm having a sandwich, so many choices to not have one. I start grabbing my ingredients when my stomach feels like it's sticking to my back, noticing the expensive cheese and meats I'm grabbing. My hands are full so I grab the bag of bread with my teeth while bumping the fridge door shut with my butt before dumping everything on the counter with a happy dance.

Just making myself at home, no biggie.

Glancing around, I grab a big knife from the knife block I spy by the chef's grill stove and swirl it between my fingers as I absentmindedly prepare the sandwich of all sand-wiches. With the knife poised over the bread to cut in half, the shine of the blade putting me in a memory that takes hold of me.

"Till, stop your whining and throw the knife. You gotta learn sometime how to handle things that are sharp before they cut you out there in the real world."

Uncle Rig once again takes me behind the junkyard, setting up wooden targets on top of the crushed cars. He's always teaching me new things, as he likes to call it 'life lessons', to survive. Don't know why knife throwing is something I need to know. He already taught me how to handle a gun at age eight and those are more useful anyway but I probably won't ever use one. I don't plan on staying in the club once I'm old enough, I'm going to go to college and meet my future husband there unless Cruz asks me to marry him. I'll just drag him with me, the guy is always glued to my side anyways. Never far from me.

"Don't you give me that look. A knife can fly through the air at a speed that is silent and that could save your life. What if I'm not around one day to protect you and you need to defend yourself?"

"Don't say that, you'll always be right here with me even when I leave this place."

"Just throw the damn knife, Till, because this could be a lesson that saves you one day." He shakes his head and watches me swirl the blade between my fingers with a happy grin full of pride. It comes naturally to me I guess.

"Fine, whatever you say, old man." The knife is flying through the air before I finish that sentence, my arm tingling from how hard I threw it but damn if I don't throw my hands in the air when the knife sticks into the wood.

My finger stings all of a sudden, bringing me out of that memory and I glance down to see I cut my knuckle with the knife. A droplet of blood pools, dripping down to my palm and I'm about to set the blade down to stop the bleeding when I hear something that sounds so familiar that my heart skips a beat. Someone is being very fucking quiet, sneaking in the dark and I know it's not Franco or his wife because I'd be able to hear their heels on the floor. Clenching the knife, I make my way around the island, following the noise of whispering voices coming from the hallway leading to the front door. A doorknob rattles with someone whispering curses on the other side like they're trying to break in.

They found me! It's too soon, I'm not prepared to end this and I'll go down fighting before they get their hands on me to drag me back to my death.

My back is plastered to the wall behind me, I swear I can hear my heartbeat pounding in my ears as I stick to the edged corner in the dark that is right outside the kitchen doorway. My ears strain for any noise and the faint sounds of footsteps coming down the hall on quiet feet, makes my hand sweaty on the grip of the knife. I try to steady my breathing by inhaling through my mouth and keeping my eyes wide open without blinking, one blink can cost me my life. A tall figure walks by dressed in all black with his boots not making a sound on the marble floors and that's my cue to come out of my hiding spot. It's now or never, these polished floors are about to be flowing red with either this fucker or mine's blood.

Ride or die is a biker saying and this girl is going to ride this blood bath with a fucking grin on my face until I'm dying to survive. I creep up behind him on the pads of my toes, coming out from the dark corner to place the knife against his back right over his kidneys which will leave the Joker bleeding a slow death.

"I'm not going back. You shouldn't have come after me because now I'm going to have to kill you." I dig the blade into the skin a little more over his shirt to prove my point that I'm not bluffing, my breath coming out in pants that I wish I could control.

This guy's whole body shudders, his shoulders shaking... is he crying? Why isn't he wearing the Joker's cut? Did Payne send another club in the area after me to do his dirty work?

"Oh, sweetness, I have to say this isn't my first time a woman threatened to kill me. Did I not call you back after fucking you into the mattress? I'm usually up front that it won't happen again after I'm done deep dicking you that you'll be feeling me for days, sweetheart." His voice softly quiet but oh so deep, just enough to give you chills that stroke down your spine.

What. The. Hell.

My grip loosens a little in shock, the pressure of the blade easing off him and he takes advantage of that as he spins around to face me. My startled breath comes out in a rush as I stare up at a face that knocks my knees together.

"Oh my, what do we have here?" He whispers in excitement as he circles around me while I try not to keep my gaze off him... as if I could even if I tried to, his blue eyes remind me of a frozen lake in the dead of winter. But oddly you can see death in his gaze too, like the grim reaper standing on the other side of the door watching but hasn't decided if he wants to take your soul or not yet.

His eyes are a mixture of blues from hot to cold, clashing together and they keep flickering to my knife then back to my face. I watch his lips spread into a slow smile as he steps closer, coming into the light of the hallway. I'm finally understanding what the lips of an angel mean. Wide, sculpted lips keep spreading across his face until a dimple appears in his right cheek and my gaze keeps going back to his lip rings that he keeps flicking with his tongue. This guy has a square face of sharp angles, giving him a beauty that almost makes it hard to look at him. Bright, blonde hair that is a mess like he runs his hand through it a lot and it's straightened so that the strands end at his perfectly defined jawline. He may look like he just stepped out of heaven, but he fell instead because no way would an angel have a smile that sinister like he plans to do very bad things... to me. He looks like he's around my age, seventeen or eighteen but everything about him screams all man from his height to the muscles straining against his black t-shirt. He gazes down at me like I'm a shiny new toy he can't wait to get his big hands on.

"Don't come any clos-closer! I don't care that you have the face of an angel, I'll gut you if I have to." My voice comes out high pitched, shaken to my core because I don't think I've seen anyone nearly as beautiful as him.

"Oh, baby, gut me." He groans out like he just came in his pants, biting his pierced lip as he looks me up and down. "Since you showed me yours, it's only fair I show you mine. If only so you know the name you'll be screaming later. It's Tey, kitten." He winks, chuckling like he's hiding a million seductive secrets that would turn a nun into the flesh of guilty pleasures.

Kitten? Why does that have my lips twitching, this guy is seriously crazy dangerous but damn if that little playful side doesn't lower my guard a little.

Must. Not. Get. Distracted.

Suddenly he bends down, making my eyes widen farther, he's standing so close and his face is right at eye level with my boobs that are practically in his face as he stares up at me before he grabs something from his black boots. A long, curved knife appears in his right hand and he brings it up to his face with the blade reflecting the light.

Does he seriously carry that in his boot? He holds my gaze as his pierced tongue flicks along the sharp end of the blade in a worshipping way that has my confused body responding, my lower lips become slick, and my panties are soaked within seconds.

What is happening to me? Why aren't I afraid like I've

always been instead of being fascinated, turned on to the point I have to keep squeezing my thighs together? He has an edge to him that makes him dangerous but his eyes sparkle with mischief and under that, I see the hard glint you only get from living a hard life. It's in my own eyes every time I look in the mirror.

CHAPTER 6

Logan

$\mathcal{M}$usic thumps through my veins with the thick cloud of smoke in the air that comes from Tey as he slumps into the couch, exhaling the stench of weed through his mouth without a care in the world. My arms clench the cushions on either side of me as I blow out a frustrated, bored breath. God, same thing, different day on an endless loop.

I. Am. Bored.

"You like that, baby?" Paris's annoying voice croons from between my legs and I roll my head down lazily until I'm staring at her kneeling position as her mouth moves up and down my dick in a sloppy mess.

Is it too much to ask for my cock to be treasured like a vanilla ice cream cone that you keep licking until you're down to the cone instead of this race she's doing in the wannabe porn Olympics? Tey chuckles next to me in amusement at my expense before reaching over and threading his black painted nails through her hair, holding the back of her head, and shoving down until she's choking on my dick. That's better but still missing something. The fucker holds her down until I actually feel a spark and releases her just as I start to feel a tingle in my spine. I watch tears leak from her eyes at being choked by my cock. She comes up gasping, coughing, and flicks her eyes to Tey with a wary look even though she smiles wobbly. She has a right to be nervous, she's just a body to be used and yet keeps coming back for more. It might be time to cut her loose before she thinks I'm going to keep her. Paris follows me around like a lost puppy, hoping to sink and hook me just because both of our parents come from money. I've fucked other girls behind her back, and plenty in front of her at parties to prove my point. She means nothing to me. Guess the dollar signs keep people around. It's a turnoff, the smell of desperation and having the same thing more than once makes me shiver because fuck that. I'm meant to taste all the flavors, not settle for one.

"You almost done there, buddy? We gotta take care of that thing. Paris, are you going to leave my boy hanging, or can you open your mouth wide to get the job done?" Tey questions lazily gesturing between us with his hand that holds a joint, bobbing his head to the music and looking relaxed from the weed in his slouched position.

Sitting in the VIP section of Toxic, one of the hottest spots in LA has its benefits, it drowns out the voices and allows us to talk business without straining to be heard over the loud music. Too fucking bad this bitch won't take the hint to leave even after telling her point blank to get the fuck out. Always on her knees even in front of my friends, she doesn't care as long as she thinks I'll put a ring on her finger one day. Like I said, desperation comes off her in waves. She only proves me right when she unzips my pants, and now I'm soft instead of being hard to the point it's almost painful.

"Poor Logan, just isn't enough anymore, is it? We need something new to toy with, maybe a new pet." Tey chuckles as he sits up, taking one more exhale before crushing the joint under his boot and blowing the smoke in Paris' face.

She coughs, looking away from him, and starts to reach for my dick again with a determined glint in her brown eyes. "Want to come on my tits instead, baby? I know you like that, I won't even clean up after so everyone knows I'm yours." She pleads up at me but I have my pants zipped up in seconds and my gun pressing against her temple. I'm a sick bastard who gets off on fear and it stinks coming out of her pores.

"Get the fuck out, Paris. You aren't mine and never will be. I don't settle for one girl. Leave before I decide to put a bullet through your skull." My tone comes out bored but I wouldn't hesitate to pull the trigger with her brain matter painting the walls.

You get raised by a monster, you become the monster, and that's exactly what I am.

"Oh no! Run, little deer, run!" Tey hollers through his laughter as she scrambles away on shaking legs like a fawn and finally fucking leaves to blend in with the rest of the writhing bodies on the dance floor.

"This shit is getting so old. Let's get the fuck out of here, go deal with that little fucking weasel and pick up the merch. My dad's going to blow a gasket if we don't stop at the precinct and get the drugs out of there before the FBI comes sniffing around." I unbutton the top of my white button down shirt with a growl of frustration, hating how restricted I feel in my tailored dress pants and classic shoes that any gentlemen should have in their closet… too bad the outfit doesn't fit who I am.

Be classy as fuck, show some dominance that matches the suit as you beat a man to death, never spill a drop of blood on your iron pressed shirt.

Tey rubs his hands together in glee next to me, winking as we pass two girls making out in the middle of the hallway trying to catch our attention.

"My brother from another mother, do you think I can check out the supplies before handing it over to dear old daddy dearest?" He smiles jokingly but under that, I can hear his need.

Tey is like a walking corpse, a little dead inside but somehow still managing to roam around. I think bouncing from foster home to foster home has fucked him up more than he lets on, his need to escape every second of the day worries me but that's why I'm here. To keep him in line so he can make it past thirty fucking years old. It's why I'm the fucking leader in our small tight knit group.

"Don't let me hear that fucking shit come out of your mouth again. The answer is no. I need your head clear for this. I'll let you take a few stabs at the warehouse to get your high."

Do I sound like a harsh bastard? Yeah, but that's just who I am. Harsh, cold but I love my boys so I'll be whoever I need to be for them. Besides, if we fuck this shit up, we are all going down until the bars slam shut and I'll be stuck in one place. That can't happen.

"You always take the fun away." He grumbles behind me but picks up his dragging feet when we exit through the back door and he rushes over to my one true love with the keys twirling on his finger.

"Not the Corvette, Tey!" I growl at him as my hand

moves lovingly over the hood of my glossy black beauty before getting into the passenger seat. "You're a shit, just don't scratch her." Might as well let him have this high adrenaline rush. The engine rumbles and Tey cranks up the music before peeling out of the parking lot.

"Fuck yeah!" He howls out the window like a fucking animal and guns it towards the warehouse so we can have some fun with the little fucktard who decided to become a traitor. Nothing like beating a man on a Saturday evening and washing your sins away Sunday morning at church.

"I'll only ask you one more time, Lenny. Where the fuck is the money?" I wipe my hands on the handkerchief that's always in my back pocket, wiping the blood away from my cracked knuckles calmly as I wait for his excuse.

"I'm telling you, I don't have the money or the missing drugs! I was just doing my job like I was told by your father. 'Take the counterfeit money from the warehouse', he said, 'deliver it and bring the coke back here!' I never ratted out to the FBI where the meth lab is, they showed up raiding the place with the SWAT team and took the drugs just before I made it down the street. I would never tell no cops!" Lenny shouts, his body trembling in the chair I tied him to not too long ago.

Tey is bouncing on his toes next to me, about to explode to cause some violence, the crazy fucker. I step back to admire my handiwork, this dumb motherfucker didn't think we'd realize that some of the supplies would slowly go missing with each shipment. Taking the drugs wouldn't be the biggest deal, maybe a few pops to his kneecaps would get our message across. But man, you messed with the wrong people thinking you can steal their money. Lenny showed up tonight at the warehouse my old man owns in the bad part of the outskirts of L.A. and actually thought it would be a brilliant idea to change out the good coke as a replacement with the bad shit that you can find on any street corner. Our stuff is pure and clean, expensive as hell, and keeps the clients coming back for more, so catching him in the act made this even sweeter. I'm not sure he was the one to pass the information to the FBI about where one of our meth labs is but something isn't adding up, so now I have to go into the station to handle it. Lenny's currently panting through each breath, could be from the broken ribs I just gave him or the blood dripping down the back of his throat from his nose that I repeatedly hit. Usually, this is Dalton's type of thing, he loves to use his fist but he's busy tonight in the underground ring, pounding the shit out of someone else at the moment.

"Let me at him, Logan! I wonder if it squeals like a pig and looks like one, if that makes him a pig? I brought my favorite knife." Tey's voice comes out as an excited purr, I wouldn't be surprised if the fucker is semi hard right now.

Lenny looks between the two of us frantically, shivering from the cold, gulping as he looks at the meat hanging from hooks in the depth of the freezer and the clear tarp hanging from floor to ceiling surrounding him. This isn't our first rodeo and I think he's finally getting it through his thick skull that the last image he'll see is skinned pigs swinging from the ceiling.

"Okay! O-kay! I'll talk! I did take a swipe of some of the blow, but that's it! I s-swear! It was only one hit. I don't know nothing about no money being taken or being a snitch to the f-fuzz," Lenny stutters, sweating like a fucking pig...How ironic. I think the guy belongs in here with the other meat, it's like destiny or something.

I exchange a look with Tey, seeing the twinkle in his eyes and we both come to the conclusion that Lenny's telling the truth. I straighten to my full height, slicking back my brown hair that hangs in my eyes, and adjust my cuffs before giving a single nod to Tey.

"Finally! This gives me the perfect opportunity to try out my artistic skills. Thank you for your tribute, I'm about to create a masterpiece," Tey whispers and without hesitation whips out his knife from God knows where and slashes across Lenny's throat.

Tey must have hit an artery because Lenny's blood squirts out of his neck like a bottle of ketchup, splatting against the clear tarp. He's fucking lucky I moved across the freezer before he started. If he got one drop of blood on my clothes, I'd have to murder him. I've been doing this for a while but I like being clean, thank you very much.

"Hurry up, we still have to get to the precinct to switch out the evidence. Fucking Lenny. If he wasn't the snitch to the FBI about the raid or missing money... looks like we have a traitor in our kingdom. Can't have that happening now, can we?"

Leaving the warehouse behind, I see out of the corner of my eye Tey wiping blood off his arms with a baby wipe while he grins the whole time over to the precinct. Rolling my eyes as we step out of my car, I toss Tey the black duffle from the trunk once we get there and he pretends to zip his lips just as we start climbing the steps into the building. The moment we slide through the doors, the noise and chaos are almost overbearing but it helps us slip by unnoticed. Phones ring off the hook, men in suits milling around barking orders while a few grab their guns and rush by us to answer a call coming through. Perfect time to pick up the supplies, there are less cops around the station once the sun goes down. Los Angeles precincts are crazy busy on a regular night and Gale, the receptionist, just waves from behind her desk when I wink at her and point towards the direction of my father's office. Nobody thinks twice about us being here because me and my boys grew up around cops with my father being Chief and all.

"Like stealing candy from a hooker." Tey chuckles as we step into the elevator and he pushes the basement level button.

"You mean from a baby, not a hooker." I roll my eyes at him, staring straight ahead as the light dings for our floor.

"Naw, hookers love their lollipops. It's how they get those tongue tricks down, my brother, I'm going to have to hire you a hooker for the night. Let's pop that cherry." He snickers under his breath and jogs ahead before I can smack him upside the head.

"Shut the fuck up and just grab the dope." My order comes out loud and clear, forcing him to be serious for the moment as I punch in the code for the evidence storage room that's full of crime scenes to drug busts.

I'm just here for the drugs.

"Case number thirty-three. Find it and switch the coke with the fake powder." I'm grumpy as hell, on constant edge because we shouldn't have to be here in the first place.

Fucking Lenny... I'll make anyone who's talking to the cops regret the day they were born.

Tey nods, swinging the bag over his shoulder with a whistle as he disappears around a shelving unit. So many cases of crimes, disaster, some unsolved, some under trial but look how easy it was for us to slip in here. Nothing but Los Angeles love in this evidence room, so much hate, and violence just like how the city is. Little do the citizens know that Franco, Chief of their beloved city, would have a hand in dealing with the most criminal cases in one form or another. Everyone is deep in his pockets, including myself. My phone won't stop vibrating against my thigh and the distracting constant messaging coming in can only be one person.

Why does he insist on calling constantly when I'm old enough to get the job done without him checking in? I answer without looking at my phone as my eyes skim over an evidence box .containing items from a brutal murder, home invasion in the suburbs.

"Chief. It's almost done, we'll be dropping the package off before-" My father interrupts me and I motion with my hands to Tey as he comes around the corner to cut off the whistling.

"Get home right the fuck now! No stopping, Logan, just get home." He commands with an authority that never fails to make me stand up straighter and harden my heart until eventually nothing will be left.

He hangs up, not letting me get in another word but that's just how it goes because he's the boss. A boss of thousands of corrupt and good police officers but also of a network of crime. He has so many people in his pockets, from the lowest ranking officer to the governor... the Chief of L.A. is untouchable.

My mama used to put him in his place, her Italian side would come out, and she grounded him whole. She was beautiful, elegant, and graceful but we all went off the deep end when she was murdered by a rival gang that Dad had to go undercover in when he was a rookie. He sent the bad guys to jail but one always slips through the cracks and it was what tore our family apart. He worked endlessly to bring our family justice but was kicked off the case because he was too close to it. He started that day at the bottom but climbed himself to the top so he could have the power where no one would even think about trying to take him down. He once said if you can't beat them, join them, and that's exactly what he did. He used to be a hero figure to the community, a police officer who wanted to make a difference, but something changed in him when Mama was lowered into the ground. He became cold hearted and turned to the other side of the law. Most fear him and respect him at the same time.

"We gotta go. I'm pretty sure my stepmom is throwing a big fucking fit again that she didn't get what she wanted." My voice comes out in a growl, I'm so sick of her shit.

Ever since my father met her, distracted by her beauty the moment she fell into his arms on the street. She snatched him away and takes his fucking money which he just turns a blind eye to. That is why I'll never fall prey to a beautiful woman who is only after one thing.

"They've been together for a few years, I honestly thought he'd get sick of the same pussy each night, but guess not. At least you got a mommy." Tey grabs his stomach, chuckling madly, thinking he's a funny comedian but we both know he'd switch places with me in a heartbeat.

He grew up in the foster system although he's spent half his childhood in my house along with Dalton and Nicky. They are my brothers even if we don't share the same blood.

"Let's just get out of here. You grab all the supplies?" I ask him as I start walking out of the evidence room with him taking his sweet time following. "No testing the goods and whatever you have in your hands, put it the fuck back."

I don't even have to bother looking, his need to steal something can get out of control unless I put him in line or

Dalton does. Usually that fucker would just sit on him until he gives up and stops trying to steal shit that can get him into trouble because it doesn't matter when or where...he'll get his sneaky fingers on anything to keep as his. I think it's abandonment issues so he takes control of something that he can call his to keep.

"Always ruining my fun, I swear, Lo. You need to get laid. Let's get this over with so I can sharpen my knives."

And he says I need to get laid? I can't even remember the last time he's had pussy. We reach the first floor, passing a bored looking Gale again, who is ten times our age but that doesn't stop her from looking at us like we're a snack. I'm a fucking dessert, not a small mussel to gobble in one bite. I'm the whole deal that makes you moan and beg for more until you're full.

"Logan Russo! Is it true that there is corruption within the law enforcement of Los Angeles and your father is well aware of the problem?" The most annoying voice speaks from behind me, her clicking heels trying to catch up to us.

"Nope! No. Not dealing with her. Make the bad thing go away Logan before I do something drastic like slit her throat. She won't be talking anymore after," Tey mumbles, and speed walks ahead of me as if he'd rather be anywhere else but here.

I couldn't agree more.

With a deep sigh, I pinch my nose and pray for patience. This fucking reporter is like a hound with a bone, somehow always sniffing me out and never goes away. She might be my number one stalker, can't tell you how many times she's shown up wherever I am. I can never tell if she wants the biggest story of her career or to hop on my big cock. Might be both. Spinning around, I confront Elle, journalist for the Los Angeles Times. All blonde, long legs in fuck me heels, big fake tits, and a woman who's always staring at me like she wants me to fuck her into next week. Practically begs for it with the way she leers at me like I'm a fucking piece of meat dangling in her face, but personally it does nothing for me, not even a twitch in the south department. There isn't a challenge, a chase, and I can only smell desperation off of her. My brow arches as she places her red nails on my bicep, squeezing my arm while licking her lips suggestively, not once noticing my hostile stare while I fantasize about snapping her neck.

"I don't talk to reporters. If you want an interview then set one up through the Chief's secretary. Would you look at the time, I have to go home and study for a history exam." I hear her huff out behind me the moment I stride away, rolling my eyes at Tey as he leans against the passenger door of my car, repeatedly grabbing the handle to try and open it.

Doesn't matter if I'm eighteen even though she's been coming around for two years, she asks questions about my family business all the while grinding against me like a cat in heat. At school, hell, even if I'm fucking around somewhere, she sniffs me out and begs me nonstop even though my answer is always the same. Blood in or nothing at all. I really don't talk to any reporters that come around, family means everything to me.

"Yessss!" Tey moans dramatically when I unlock my car and hop in with a relieved breath.

He immediately looks at his phone when it starts buzzing with a lot of incoming texts, the blue light highlighting his face, his icy blue eyes wide with a look I know all too well. Lorenzo. King of putting together illegal street races. It switches from place to place and invites only.

"When and where?" The yearning is clear in my voice. I

try to hide it but when you grow up around someone your whole life they tend to know when you're faking it.

We haven't heard from Lorenzo in weeks and my hands clench the wheel as a need overcomes me, like a hunger that can't be satisfied until I'm feeling the rush. My hands were meant to steer, take control, and push past limits that break the law. Nicky and I haven't been in a street race in months, something we both need like the air in our lungs. Tey always collects bets and gets the crowd going with Dalton standing over him like a shadow in case shit goes down. Lorenzo puts the street races together, knowing fuckers that will pay to see rubber burn. The man knows how to get just the right people that will place bets, handing over their money like it's nothing and in these parts, it's really not a big deal.

"Two weeks from now, starting right fucking downtown to Chinatown!" His voice shakes me out of my thoughts in the quiet exterior of the car and we're already pulling into the community lined with mansions on both sides of the street in no time at all.

"Tell him we'll be there and to make sure he has his money ready." A smile spreads across my face as I scratch my five o'clock shadow to hide my smirk but Tey chuckles like he knows what I'm thinking.

Flicking off the headlights, I wave Tey ahead to go inside to raid the fridge like he always does while I switch the bags to my father's car and mentally prepare to deal with the lashing I'll get for allowing this to happen in the first place under my watch. I didn't know the fucking runner aka Lenny would be sampling the goods, getting high as fuck, and letting the meth house get raided.

Slamming the trunk of the Aston Martin my father drives around, as if a chief could afford this, I wonder if life would have taken a different turn if Mom was still alive. If my father wouldn't have become the fucking mafia. It's still in the back of my mind that one day I'll wake up and see Mom and Dad eating breakfast in our little home just on the outskirts of L.A. Don't get me wrong, I like who the hell I am now, it's all I know, and the power that comes with it is like oxygen.

Addicting and yearning.

I walk through the garage door quietly, already prepared for my dad to ask for an update, instead I stop in my tracks to see Tey towering over a girl in the doorway of the kitchen. Her back is turned towards me, giving me a view of an ass that's round and fucking biteable, encased in a tight pair of shorts that should be illegal because her legs look like they go on for miles. They'd look better around my waist.

Her hair hangs down in wet, dark ropes with a hint of purple down to the curve of her ass but what really holds my attention is the flash of metal I see in her hand. She's gripping that knife handle pretty tight as Tey bends down to retrieve his baby from his boot. It's almost cute, is she trying to threaten him with that tiny weapon? It's a kitchen blade for fucks sake.

Who is this delectable creature and why is she in my fucking house? Did my dad hire a stripper? She has the body for it, all the right curves, and my hands itch to touch her skin where her pulse is pounding, to feel the beat under my palm as I wrap my hand around her neck and demand control over her. It's almost laughable and I doubt my dad would bring a stripper home, pretty sure I'd hear the stepmom screeching like a banshee if that happened.

My feet move across the kitchen on deadly quiet intent and she freezes when she feels me pressing up along her body from behind, taking her knife quickly from her grip and flinging it across the kitchen where it embeds into a cabinet. The smell of rain, sweet vanilla, and I swear sunshine reaches me when I bend down to skim my nose along the curve of her neck. The shiver that runs through her body makes me smile and I glance at Tey whose own eyes fill with lust as he runs the blade down her cheek at the same time.

We are sick, twisted bastards that find pleasure in the dark that bleeds the night against smooth honeyed skin just as soft as hers. She hasn't looked away from Tey or screamed, it says a lot about her if she can deal with this level of psycho. I actually don't like it because she's distracting me when I should be pulling out my gun and finding out why she's in my house. Maybe she's been sent by another gang to get the drop on us and that sobers me somewhat.

"I think you're in the wrong house, baby girl. Unless you're here to give us a little show. Tey, you hired a stripper? I'm flattered. It's not even my birthday." She gasps in outrage as Tey chuckles darkly and quickly spins around in my arms to confront me, her hands gripping my biceps as she looks up at me with anger and shock written on her face.

My gaze is drawn to lips that are a pale pink, plump, and shaped as the perfect O right now as her mouth hangs open.

"Logan! It's like destiny, man!" Tey's eyes are turning a dark blue and I know he wants her too. "You want to play with us…" He trails off from behind her, waiting for her name but she's a stuttering mess between us.

"How did you know- No! I'm not here to entertain you with stripping you fucking perve. Back the hell away!" She digs her nails into my skin, and instead of pushing me away she only holds on tighter.

She closes her eyes for a second as if to pray for patience but it only gives me time to study her without actually having her see how she's putting me off my game. Long, dark lashes frame her high cheekbones, her skin looks soft as fuck, and her dark eyebrows scrunch together in confusion, forming a tiny wrinkle that I, for some reason, find adorable. She snaps her eyes open when Tey presses up against her from behind tightly, caging her in between our bodies. The anger that flares in her dark chocolate eyes has my cock straining against my dress pants and she realizes a moment later when my hardening length grazes along her stomach. Her head just barely reaches my bicep. Tey and I are both looking down at her small frame, standing over six feet. God, she's absolutely perfect and it pisses me off. My eyes flicker quickly to Tey above her head with a silent message to figure out what she's doing here. He nods and slides her hair over her other shoulder to expose her swan-like neck. He groans out in ecstasy when he skims the flat of the blade down her neck and towards her shoulder. I watch as she holds her breath looking up at me but yet she's not running or screaming like a normal person would. Has a blade touched baby girl before? I can't wait to find out.

I stare down at her with my head tilted as I try to figure her out, gazing into her dark eyes that shine under the dim lights but under that, I see a ghost. It's a past that haunts you, stays with you, and fucks you up in the head so that it's hard to tell what's right or wrong.

"Why aren't you taking off your clothes already? It's what you're hired to do right? Make it slow, baby girl, give us a show." My gaze flicks up and down her exquisite body, pretending to find her lacking when in reality she burns me alive like a flick of a match.

Her breathing picks up, her breasts heaving up and down against my abs and she reaches back without taking her eyes off me. She grasps the blade from over her shoulder faster than I was expecting, taking the flat of the blade between her thumb and index finger, sliding it from Tey's grip before he knows what happened. I'm not the least bit surprised when she holds it under my jugular with fury blazing across her face, her gorgeous lips curving up in a snarl that turns me the fuck on.

Have I ever been this turned on to the point of it being painful? Like my cock needs to sink into her warm pussy and stay there, buried deep until the floodgates are open and she's praising my name.

Nope.

I bet Tey is thinking the same thing because when she switches hands to hold the handle of the knife in a tight grip, he grabs her bleeding hand that was cut from the sharp edge of the blade she made in her grab. She watches out of the corner of her eye and bites her bottom lip down hard as Tey placed his lips against the small nick and runs his tongue along the dripping trail of blood with a devious grin on his face.

"Hmm, I'm going to make you scream until your voice is hoarse. I just bet you're flexible, I can't wait to find out how much," Tey mutters quietly, his pupils dilated and she starts trembling between us, her wide eyes reflecting with the same hunger I feel in my own gut.

"Keep dreaming, pretty boy. You won't be getting any of this and you don't scare me. I've already met the devil and you have nothing on him." She lifts her chin, teeth grinding, and her voice comes out sweet yet raspy with anger.

We can't have that, now can we. The look of displeasure and indifference directed at us has my palm twitching. I'd like nothing more than to drag her over my knee and spank her ass red until she's begging for more.

"Logan, Tey, get the fuck away from her. That's not any

way to treat our guest." My head snaps up at my father's voice as he comes around the corner from the hallway that leads to his office, taking in the scene with a calculating gaze in his eyes.

Baby girl slips out from between us faster than I'd like, taking her delicious warmth with her that I didn't know I was craving. Tey actually pouts, snatching his knife back from her grip with ease and looking at it with a light in his eyes that makes me worried for his sanity. He slips it back into his boot with a sigh while she backs away towards the front entrance, keeping her eyes on us as if she's planning on running. Bad move, never run from the bad guy, we love the chase. A challenge really. And I do love a good challenge, but her timing is off. A drug bust just happened the other night, a leak in the system, and yet here is this girl who appears innocent as fuck on the outside with her heart shaped face and big, chocolate eyes that suck you in, but something dark is hidden underneath, just full of secrets waiting to be told.

"Tillie, please excuse my son's behavior. I swear he wasn't raised by a pack of wolves. Why don't you take the guest room on the other side of the house, you must be exhausted and we can talk in the morning when my wife is feeling better?" My father may sound like he's giving her a choice but his narrowed eyes say it's not up for discussion.

"Yes. Don't go running off in the night, where it's dark with monsters out there that would love to take a bite out of you." I smirk at her, chomping my teeth once, and watch her chin rising with confidence but her throat bobs as she looks between us all.

"Please run, please," Tey whispers in anticipation under his breath and she hears him, eyeing him before she glares as if she's thinking of ways to murder us.

Why do I like that thought?

"I wouldn't want to overstay my welcome and I hope your wife is feeling better in the morning. There's so much I need to know. I won't be in your hair much longer after I get answers," baby girl says quietly, refusing to look away from my father's gaze as he slowly nods.

I've seen that look before, she's not going anywhere because he doesn't trust her. Keep your enemies close.

What the hell is going on?

"Whatever you want, I'm sure your- Diana would want you to stay. I'll show you to the guest room." He walks over to her, grabbing her black duffle that I didn't notice a few feet away, and starts to stride out of the room without a backward glance to see if she's following.

She stands frozen, her face drained of color and she looks almost scared to follow him alone in the dark. I don't like that, she had a fire in her eyes minutes before as she stared up at me.

"Don't want to keep him waiting. Unless you'd rather come over here and put that mouth to better work." My meaning is clear as I take a step forward.

She glares and stomps past me to follow my father down the dark hallway, her ass swinging side to side, an ass that I'd like to take a bite of. In due time, and then I'll toss her aside like I always do to every woman that tries to get close to me.

"Nighty night, pet." Tey chuckles amused but his head is tilted to the side with his gaze glued to her ass too, staying there until she turns a corner towards the other side of the house.

Why is it easier to breathe once she's gone from the room?

"I'm going to keep her," Tey says with a gleam in his eyes that's all too familiar.

"And then destroy her," I reply back knowingly because that's just what we do when pretty things step into our lives, they don't stay innocent once we have a taste... there isn't any going back. You've been marked, tainted by evil, and coming back to sin again and again because you can't help yourself to have one more taste.

This one won't be any different.

CHAPTER 7

Tillie

"*You thought you could escape me? You'll never get away, I'll always find you because I own you,*" *Cruz whispers into my ear but I can't see him. It's so dark. An abyss but his voice seems to be everywhere at once. He's right, I can't escape from something I can't even see.*

"*I'm coming.*" *He's suddenly in front of me with chains in his bloody hands and the sound of them snapping around my wrists with an echo has my lungs desperately working to get air in. "I'm here.*"

A loud gasp wakes me up, making me realize I was the one to make the noise and throwing me out of my nightmare. My head smacks against the bedroom door I slept against all night, I don't trust anyone and wasn't going to let my guard down to be vulnerable ever again. My eyes swing around the room and my shoulders sag when I realize I'm in a guest bedroom right across from Satan's room. I now understand the meaning where they say he fell from heaven, his beauty indescribable but angelic. Honey eyes that look past the outer layer of skin and see the inside to only take you apart piece by piece with his gaze. I bet he's a man who cuts you open just to see if he was right and doesn't bother to sew you back up.

Logan.

Tall, drop dead gorgeous, and dangerous. I read all that in seconds when our eyes connected as he towered over me, looking down as if I'd caused him physical harm but also he wanted to drag me away and lock the door as he watches me suffer before giving me what I need.

I'm not sure what exactly my body needs but when the guy dressed from head to toe in black with the smile of madness, dragged a blade down my neck, I didn't feel like my life was in danger. I felt like he was playing a game but wouldn't hurt me, only bring me so high that I would never want to come back down. I had to escape before they sucked all the air out of the room, tearing off my wet panties with their teeth without even trying. Logan's father is just as intense as his son, both men who can set the world on fire and not care as everyone perishes in the flames. He looked at me with calculating eyes, not trusting me which makes him a smart man. A stranger comes into his home, in the middle of the night, soaking wet from the downpour, and begging to find a safe place even if it's only for a little while. Hell, I'm still covered in dirt, a cut on my leg visible and my clothes stiffly sticking to my body. He must be nuts since he walked said stranger, that's me, to their guestroom, opening the door to a room that made my jaw drop and said good freaking night.

Okay, he didn't say that, more like, *"This is where you will be sleeping, Tillie, hope you're comfortable and have a goodnight's sleep. I'll make sure the doors are locked up tight."*

Franco smiled tightly and raised a brow at me as if to say don't think about leaving. I'll be watching.

Message loud and clear buddy.

So I scoped out the room the minute the door was shut and this is how I came to be. A crick in my neck, a sore ass that fell asleep on the dark wood floor even though the king sized bed looked inviting... no way was I sleeping with my back turned towards the door where anyone could come in. My body blocked all access especially from the two men that spelled trouble. I heard footsteps coming down the hall last night as I was dozing off, stopping right on the other side, and a light tapping against the wood.

"Night, sugar, dream of me. Naked would be best if you're having a nightmare, at least it's something hot to look at."

Tey chuckled darkly as Logan's honeyed voice told him to leave the stray alone. He's not completely wrong, I am a stray. No place to call home, a desperate girl just trying to live.

Stretching my hands over my head, I grimace as the cut on my leg burns from the motorcycle accident. Looking down, it's not bleeding but it looks a tad angry on my calf. I'll be so pissed if I've come this far to die from an infection. Glancing around with clearer eyes, the sun peaks through the billowing white curtains that draw me closer to look on the other side. French doors lead to an Italian brick balcony right outside my room on the second floor, and down below is a pool glistening under the California sunshine that is almost as big as the mansion. This is completely opposite of what I'm used to and it kind of freaks me out, turning away from the window, I take a look around the guest bedroom I'm calling mine for now. Dark wood floors with a light grey rug that the bed sits on, a white bed frame with sheer drapes that wrap around the banisters and gives the illusion of privacy. My small, duffle bag looks pathetic in the walk-in closet with only two outfits I have to my name. I really don't fit in with this rich lifestyle but at least I can clean up my appearance before hitting the road again and finding somewhere I can disappear for good.

The shower is calling my name, with blood and dirt covering me with layers that even the rain couldn't wash away, so it would probably be best if I clean up before heading downstairs with a fake smile.

Opening the door opposite of the closet reveals the bathroom, this is what dreams are made of. Glossy, black marble floor, a huge tub to fit at least five people, a standing walk-in shower with multiple shower heads, and floor to ceiling tinted windows that overlooks the lush acres of green grass. I've never seen grass that green and once again the wonders of having money blow my mind. That has to be extremely expensive especially living in California.

What the hell did I walk into? A closed door across the bathroom has a lock, I quickly snap it into place because I'm pretty sure this is a Jack and Jill bathroom but I'm not taking the chance of Satan walking in on me naked.

My face in the mirror makes me gasp out loud, the way I look right now makes me question if the people living in this house are butt ass crazy. I really do look like a drowned rat with my hair knotted and sticking up in every direction, my clothes wrinkled and sticking to my body like a dirty second skin. Clothes fly across the room as I struggle to get out of them in a fight to the death. Breathing heavily from my struggle, I twist the knob for the water to be so scolding hot that it feels like the Devil is licking my skin with his hot tongue.

I will not think of that hothole Logan licking me. The last thing I need in my life is a man controlling me. That man had a possessive gleam in his gaze last night that didn't frighten me. It made me burn. Seeing his honeycomb eyes filled with enough shadows like my own, it called to me, sucked me right in and I let it take hold without the thought of it hurting. Maybe I've been through so much that I'm finally taking the leap to live even when it feels like I'm going to have a heart attack.

Stepping under the hot spray eases my shoulders and melts me on the spot from all the showerheads beating down on me, washing away my past one step at a time. I wonder what it was like growing up like this, not having to worry about if you'll make it to eighteen or eventually being forced to live on the streets.

I reach for the shampoo on the built-in shelves since I don't have any in my duffle bag, the smell drawing me in. It reminds me of breathing in a forest for the first time, pine trees with that fresh smell only nature can bring. A smile easily spreads across my face as I lather my hair with my eyes closed and tilt my head back to rinse off. I freeze with my hands threaded in my hair when the shower stall door silently opens, my eyes popping open in shock as Logan steps under the spray opposite of me. He just stares with those intense, honey eyes and leans around me to grab the body wash without looking away from my widening eyes.

I can't move, hardly breathe. I've never been this exposed in front of a man without him wanting something from me or just taking it, but Logan just stands there watching me like it's no big deal we are showering together as he washes his body. The suds trail down his olive tone skin, making my pulse pound away as he rinses off under the spray. It's at that moment I realize my hands are still in my hair, back arched and my breasts thrust out. Quickly dropping my arms, I cross them over my chest and start backing away.

"What's wrong, baby girl? Are you afraid of me? Nothing I haven't seen before." He smirks as he looks me up and down as if he finds me lacking.

My tattoos make me self conscious under his stare with my scars that are somewhat hidden behind the ink. My legs and arms are ink free but most of my back is covered, trailing its way around to my front to cover the knife wounds that were carved into my skin like an oil painting. My ribs are cursive designs of quotes and images that remind me of finding peace one day. Ride or die is scarred into my skin just below my right breast in cursive while the rest is swirling ivy vines displayed with butterflies and flowers that always captured my attention when I saw them in magazines. His eyes linger on them now, drawn back to them again and again with a sneer on his face that highlights his sharp cheekbones. He makes that disgusted face towards me look good.

I hate him already.

He smooths the curls on top of his head back, making his hair appear a dark brown as it's slicked out of his face, and droplets of water cling to his long lashes as he stares down at me. I can't help looking as his biceps flex, my eyes are drawn to his sculpted body of tight muscles. I've never seen a man so absolutely... strong and hard edges. Capable with lean but big hands, muscles that shift and strain each time he moves. His hand smooths down his chest as he continues watching me, moving down to wash his cut abs in slow movements that draw my gaze, just like he wanted. I can't help eating him up which surprises me because honestly, I thought I was dead inside, that I would never be able to feel anything, but right now, by the swollen, needy feeling between my legs... I like what I see, a lot.

Those strong hands lead further down past his hips that

form a perfect V, and down to a cock that makes me swallow hard. I can't tell if I'm frightened or in awe because even his cock is perfect. Long, and thick with a slight curve that it almost scares me because that thing would wreck my insides from the angle and depth but it makes me rub my thighs together the longer I stare. Right about now is when I usually go into defense mood, blacking out eventually as he has his way with me and panic sets in but no more. I'm done being used, abused by men, it's time I start fighting back because what else is there to live for if you're really not living?

His chuckle helps me look away quickly, blood rushing to my cheeks and pissing me the fuck off. He doesn't have to do anything but stand there looking like God created him slowly, taking his time to make sure each part of him was made to cause pleasure. He's going to make my life a living hell, I don't need a man. All they've ever done is cause me pain, he can't be any different.

"I'm not afraid of you. Oh, honey, didn't you know?" I ask seductively, making sure my voice is raspy to lure him in just like I was taught to capture a man's attention.

He tilts his head in confusion, his eyes darkening with lust as I step back into the water and grab the body wash from him to leisurely wash my body without a care in the world. Little does he know how fast my heart is beating and my legs wanting to collapse underneath me in fear. I don't get the feeling, he wants to hurt me physically but more mentally. Don't get me wrong, the vibes he's throwing at me scream dangerous but oddly I'm not running.

"Know what?" He asks in a distracted, husky voice, he can't keep his eyes off me even if he tried.

My hands move down my neck with the water flowing over me, trailing slowly down to my collar bone and pausing for a heartbeat in dangerous excitement before gliding the fingertips of my hands down to my breasts with each shallow breath. I like this, making him want me when clearly he's fighting it.

I'm. In. Control.

I hold his stare when his molten honeycomb eyes flicker up to mine, the pupils expanding until I'm falling into them. A moan vibrates around the shower, making me realize it's my own mouth opening, releasing those noises the longer I rub in circles around my areola until my nipples harden under his heated but pissed off gaze.

It's exhilarating, playing with fire and almost hoping to get burned.

Peeking up at him from under my lashes, I bite my lip to stifle my moan because it's obvious he likes what he sees and hears but hates how it's affecting him at the same time. With his nostrils flaring, his fists opening and closing, it tells me enough how bad he wants me. I don't stop touching myself, he wants me, and I'm definitely playing with fire; when will he burn for me as much as I am for him? It's empowering and makes me feel like I have control of something I've never had before... I'm fucking horny, starving to be cherished. Pure, mutual lust that we are both fighting against even when our bodies sway towards each other.

I can only hear the water pelting the tilted floor and our heavy breathing filling the steamed shower, making it appear as if the outside world doesn't exist. Maybe he'll pretend a little bit more with me so the darkness stays away until I'm spinning in circles and he grounds me into reality.

"Know that you haven't seen anyone like me before." It's my turn to smirk as I finally respond back to him, turning the tables as I spin around to wash off, giving him a view of my messed up back.

Dismissing him without a care that I know will piss him off because he commands attention just by walking into a room. I'll just keep acting like this is normal and I shower in front of men all the time.

Am I prepared for his next actions? Fuck no. I'm completely caught off guard and hardly know myself, I secretly love every dirty second. This is what desire should feel like, of wanting something so bad that you'll drop to your knees and beg to keep feeling it.

A deep growl of pure male lust and anger kisses down my spine just before his scalding, hot body is plastered against my back as he grips a fist full of my wet hair and tips my head back until I'm looking up at his tense face upside down.

"You may be right, baby girl, but this is my house, my rules, and I don't fuck around. I don't trust you and just know I'll be watching every move you make. Every breath that escapes your sexy lips, every mutter under your breath while you're sleeping, I'll be there to listen; which is kind of cute when you talk in your sleep by the way." His smirk is anything but teasing.

He wants me to know that he can get into my room without even trying and he was watching me sleep last night.

This fucker must have watched my pathetic ass sleep against the bedroom door and he probably laughed because I was stupid to not even think about the joining bathroom access into my guest room.

"You tease the beast and he comes back biting, baby girl." His voice is a seductive whisper along the curve of my jaw, pulling me in closer under his spell.

His mouth swallows my gasp of outrage before I can tell him off but it's forgotten as I get a taste of intoxicated sin that surprisingly tastes like dark chocolate. Something that makes you take your time to savor the flavor, devouring more because you know it's not the worst thing but still not the healthiest for you. His tongue sweeps in, gliding against mine with a smoothness that has me reaching, arching my spine to tangle my hand in his curly hair and dragging him closer against my back. I can feel his hard cock digging into my lower back, leaving me breathless. A chill sweeps up my spine, for once not from being scared but turned the fuck on.

He breaks away, his chest heaving as he stares down at me without saying anything for a split second, watching for something that I'm not quite sure what he's looking for but my body knows. His lips curl in a snarl just as he trails his other hand down my spine, stopping just above my ass before applying slight pressure.

"Bend the fuck over," he commands, his voice gravelly and deep that shoots straight to my pussy, making me squeeze my eyes shut as something blossoms tightly in my lower stomach like a wonderful drug that makes heat spread through me.

My eyes snap back open when I feel his hard cock, long and thick pulse against the curve of my ass as he bends down slightly. Freaking hell, this is probably going to hurt but I want it. I'm going to dissolve into hot, molten lava if he doesn't do anything soon. The edge of my mind yells at me to run until my feet hit the ocean, and keep going until only my head is above the surface.

He just continues to stare, waiting, giving me a way out of this but... I. Need. This.

It's crazy, wild, and something I've never had, it's all in the palm of my hands.

I release my hands from his hair, reaching in front of me

to place the palms of my hands on the cold tile, I slowly bend over without looking away from him over my shoulder. His fingers tangle deeply into my hair, sliding through my strands slowly before holding tight in a firm grip as he pulls until my head is tilted back and my back arches under the pressure. I can't move without it stinging. His other hand slides over my wet skin, tracing my tattoo of a fairy with huge wings on my back, leaving behind a trail of heat that causes goosebumps to break out and my breathing picks up in rushed excitement. I don't know what I'm doing but the need is too great. It's everything.

"Now what?" My voice is barely recognizable, raspy, and needy.

A dark eyebrow arches like he's confused, my own arching in response like I know what I'm talking about. His gaze trails over my body as he hums in the back of his throat in pleasure, as if he likes what he sees even though I know he'd rather not show it.

It's funny, I don't know Logan. Not for even one day but my body feels like I've known him for forever, that he can play me like a violin even when my chords are broken.

"Now I'm going to ruin you, damage you inside and out until all you know is the shape of my cock and only mine." He states matter of factly, looking down at me just as he lines his cock at my pussy entrance and plunges in without warning.

A startled gasp leaves my mouth as I brace myself more firmly against the wall, my heels leaving the shower floor as he bottoms out, his dick stretching me past its limits and my pussy flooding with wetness. In and out, he moves slowly, letting me get used to his big cock until my moan bounces off the walls.

"You're so tight, baby girl. Like you were made for my

cock. I'm going to rearrange your insides, pushing my cock until you feel me for days after," he whispers in my ear. Pulling my head back further, he kisses me deeply upside down, as if he is sealing everything. "Are you ready for more?" He mutters against my lips, leaving an inch of space between us as he slides his cock out until he's right at my opening before sliding back inside just as unhurried.

He makes me feel every glide, my pussy juices drip down my thigh, and I should be embarrassed but it feels too damn good as I clench around him with small spasms that leave my legs shaking and feeling weak in the knees.

"M-more?" I breathe out, gasping loudly and his lips spread into a lopsided smirk against mine just before he crosses his one arm between my breasts and his strong fingers wrap around my throat, lifting me until my back is plastered to his chest, straining in his hold.

Fingers leave my hair, sliding so slowly down my body until stopping at my hip bone and gliding across my sensitive skin downward in a feather light touch until he applies pressure just above my pubic bone. My eyes roll into the back of my head the moment he drags his hips away and only slamming back inside in a powerful thrust that jolts me forward. The feeling of him deeper overwhelms me and causes me to shove my ass back against him with a silent plea for more.

"Give me more, I can take it. I want it," I moan loudly, unable to help myself.

He doesn't waste meeting my demand as he continues thrusting in and out like his life depends on it. His strong fingers clasp around my throat, tightening until each breath is a struggle but I love it as I push my ass back faster to meet him thrust for hard thrust because I'm racing towards something that has my pussy clamping down on him with liquid heat pulsing through me.

His groan is loud and drawn out, he's just as affected, loving every second. The sharp sting against my ass surprises me, leaving me tense for a split second until I realize how good it feels. The noise gets louder and louder with each quick slap against my ass cheeks making my skin red, and my breath short from his hand gripping around my windpipe. But my body likes it, my wet pussy coating him, and making it easier to fuck me into next week. For a split second my eyes close, only darkness surrounding me in a place that haunts me every waking second, bringing back a past that's trying to break through until his voice drags me to the surface with a desperate gasp leaving my mouth wide open as if I'm drowning.

"Tell me you're mine. That you're my slut and this pussy is only mine to destroy," he demands in a deep voice. One hand sliding around to my front and circling my clit in fast movements with his fingertip just as his other hand tightens enough to cut off my air supply with his arm still holding me up, my toes barely graze the tiled floor.

"Your slut," I manage to breathe out with a choked gasp, my vision blurring as he really fucks me with hard, rough movements, his cock dragging along something inside me that has my stomach clenching and my pussy fluttering around him in endless spasms of cruel pleasure.

I only say it's cruel because I didn't know it could be this way. It's an out of body experience, someone else taking control of my body and making me feel everything all at once. It doesn't cause me to drift away into another place and time, just the here and now of ecstasy.

"Now be a good girl and fucking come," he whispers low in my ear just like the devil, pounding so hard into me that it sets my body off and he releases my neck at the same time but I hardly notice as my whole body shakes, an orgasm tearing through me.

"Fuck. Did you just squirt?" He groans in lustful agony and pulls out of me in a flash to drop his hold on me, spinning my body around to face him in seconds flat.

His chest is heaving up and down rapidly like he just ran a mile, staring with dilated pupils, all I can see is black in his gaze. It lets me know that he wants me with a passion that could set the world on fire and rain couldn't put us out.

Who is Logan? The man holding me up right now as I try to catch my breath and focus my world back as it just reached fucking heaven. I just had an orgasm that burst from me, coating his dick as my body jerked against him as I kept coming and coming. Yeah, I fucking squirted, I didn't even know that was possible. I thought it was made up because the sweetbutts used to gossip back in the club that it was for fairytales unless you found a real man. Guess it just took the right guy.

I want more. It's like a drug, the need to keep shooting up until I have my fill. If I was to have an addiction, this would be it. Logan's cock. Funny how I have feelings for him without knowing him but it feels... normal, which is new for me.

I can't think straight, my body shaking, my knees knock together as he places his hands on my shoulders and pushes me to the ground in a silent command. He runs the pad of his thumb over my bottom lip, not anything but everything with his eyes that say he wants me. The cooling water runs over my face, making me blink rapidly up at him as I wait for his instructions. Can this never stop? I want to feel, to be able to know what it feels like to be wanted and desired without it being forced.

Logan steps forward, releasing my bottom lip, and waits for me to make up my mind if I want to suck him off or not. I think of how he just made me see stars, gave me pleasure for the first time in my life, and is patiently waiting without making me do shit that I'm uncomfortable with. I think this guy deserves an award and it's going to be my first time sucking on a cock that I put in my mouth without it shoving past my tightly shut lips. Breathing through my nose, I slowly open my mouth wide until the corner of my lips burn and sit back on my heels with a shiver diving down my spine in delight at his grunt of approval. He steps closer, looking down at my upturned face with his teeth clenched before smiling in arrogance. Can he tell I've never done this before? Yeah, we can't have that. I'll show him just how good I can be.

Without a warning, I lean forward and take half of him into my mouth, my lips stretching with a pleasurable burn around his length. He hisses out a breath and weaves his fingers through my hair in a tight hold. It shouldn't feel good but it does. I draw back slowly to swirl my tongue around him like a lollipop, lapping at the taste of our combined passion with an eagerness that has him thrusting his hips to get back into my mouth. With short, teasing bobs, I quickly take him whole in one go until he hits the back of my throat. I feel his cock jump on my tongue as I swallow, humming in pleasure and pulling back slightly before going back down on him until he's thrusting into my mouth with unabandoned control. With a guy who loves control, power... to see him come undone turns me on to the point that I hardly recognize myself. I look up at him through my lashes to see him already staring down at me with his lips parted just before his head tilts back. He lets out a loud groan that echoes around the shower and starts to come in thick ropes down my throat. I breathe through my nose, my eyes watering as I try not to gag as he forces his hips forward. Jets of cum coat my tongue that I quickly swallow and pull back until just the tip of him is left in my mouth, I lick him completely clean. He steps back on a stumble, his fists clenched at his side and I'm surprised by the cruel expression on his face as he stares down at me.

"How much?" He asks, his expression smooths out until it's impossible to read him.

On shaking legs, I stand up with a gasp, backing up the angrier he gets as the silence eats its way between us.

"How much, what?" My voice comes out small, shaken, and I want to slap myself at how vulnerable I sound.

Weak.

His face twists into a smile that has me shrinking inside myself because it's straight up ignorant and nasty.

"How much do I owe you? I mean it wasn't the best I've ever had, but I'm sure if you keep practicing sucking dick you'll get better at it." He shrugs, turning off the shower, and opens the stall door while grabbing a towel to dry off as I stand there with water dripping down my body.

Owe me? As in... no he can't possibly mean as a cheap prostitute? The possessive ownership when he dirty talked in my ear, the control he handed over even when he was in charge allowed me to let go of everything, to just be. Please don't take this one good moment away from me!

Don't ruin this!

Tears gather at the corner of my eyes but I quickly blink them away before he can see and straighten my spine because I won't be treated as if that meant nothing when I know he felt the same connection I was grabbing with desperate fingers. If he wants to start a war, then so be it. I'm done being the person left at the curb, treated like garbage and someone forgettable. He won't forget me after this, I'll be his every thought every morning and before he falls asleep, while I'll forget he ever existed in the first place.

"That was free, only because I couldn't stand the desperate stench coming off of you. That was a pity fuck, asshole." I'm proud of myself for how emotionless I sound, the evidence of pain gone from me even though it feels like a hole was punched through my chest and I'm still bleeding.

I step out of the shower without even bothering to look at him, walking naked to my guest bedroom door with my head held high. The silent prayer coming from my lips goes unnoticed by him, I catch his expression in the mirror as I pass by. If looks could kill, I'd be six feet under already and rotting in an unmarked stone cold grave.

Don't cry, don't let him see how damaged you really are.

I'm already in the doorway when his quiet voice reaches me, knowing I've been marked and targeted as a threat.

"I wouldn't get too comfortable, baby girl, people around here end up disappearing without a trace. I'll be watching and I will find out why you're really here." His tone says it all, he won't hesitate to kill me even though he just fucked me.

What kind of world have I stepped into? After leaving one full of violence behind, it seems to follow me no matter where I go. The door slams behind me as he stomps off to his room, his anger seeping into my bones with a chill. I'm not going to die after finally fighting back. I'll find out why Doris sent me here, then I'm leaving like the devil is whipping at my heels.

CHAPTER 8

Nicky

"Do not disgrace this family, Son. You do your job and watch out for your little, damaged sister. You would do well to remember that. You can leave now." Jin, head of the family and gang of the Triads; the most feared criminal gang in downtown Chinatown, and also known as my father. He orders me away without looking up from the supply of cocaine on his desk as he weighs each wrapped package. He passes the drugs to the two girls who are down to their underwear without blinking an eye. It's normal to see half naked woman around here, human trafficking isn't anything new and it really disgusts me how he treats people. Am I going to turn into him by the time the family business is placed in my hands? Will I treat my sister as if she's a disgrace or when it's time for me to claim a bride...will my heart be so cold that not even she can break through?

His order is a daily reminder that if I fail my family, I

better start running because if I'm caught, I'll just be another body found in a dumpster behind one of the diners in Chinatown.

"Yes, Father." I bow at the waist and straighten when he clears his throat in a dismissal.

Quickly spinning on my heels to exit his office, I keep my facial expression neutral as I pass his guards that glare daggers at me.

Don't show your anger, no emotions.

I hate when my father talks about my baby sister that way, she can't help that she has Tourettes... it's what makes her special and unique in my eyes.

I shake off the rage creeping to the surface, ignoring the way my father's guards place a hand on their guns. They would like nothing better than to see me dead, not liking the idea of me taking my father's place one day, making me in charge. I'd rather not have anything to do with it either, but when you're forced into this world, there is no escaping. You're born into it and you die in it.

I glance at my watch, checking the time only to see that I'm late to head over to Logan's. I received a short text last night from him telling me to come right over in the morning, and that shit was going down. At first, I thought it was about the package of drugs from the station downtown that went wrong, but he would have told me to come over right away last night if that was the case. It's something else, once again this world doesn't ever sleep and it's one thing after another. I've known Logan since elementary school, our mutual brutal households tying us together, and our friendship never bugged our fathers. They practically pushed our friendship the moment they found out. Father says that the crime families should stay together, good for business, but to never forget that everyone is an enemy and to trust no one, even your best friends. Tey and Dalton have had their fair share of cruelty, it's what brought us all together.

Swinging my car keys around my finger, I finally relax with a grin on my face as my sweet precious comes into view under the parking garage. My racing machine, she's a beauty and the only woman I will ever need in my life without the mess that comes with it. Sliding onto the leather seat, I shudder with the pressure off my shoulders as she roars to life underneath me. I need to race, and very soon, before I lose control... again.

Racing out of the garage, I pass restaurants decorated with bright colors, of golds and reds with the smell of food heavy in the air. Streets pass in a blur as I weave through Los Angeles traffic, shifting the clutch to speed down the highway, the engine purring like a kitten. This is heaven. Unfortunately, all too soon, I'm pulling up to Logan's father's mansion and killing the engine to sit in the driveway for a couple of seconds to collect my thoughts before stepping into chaos as usual.

With a sigh, I slide out of the car slowly, and shut the door behind me. I jog up the steps with my sunglasses shielding my eyes and the deepening bruise covering my left eye. Martial arts last night was brutal, my father was yelling in the background for his instructor to push me harder, hit harder, until every muscle in my body was straining. I don't bother knocking on the front door, I just let myself in like I own the damn place. I walk into silence, only to see Tey laying in the living room on the rug as he stares up at the ceiling with a wicked smile on his face. What is that crazy fool up to now?

"Nicky, my man, you won't believe what we have hiding in this house. Spectacular beauty and I can't wait to play with her," Tey mutters happily under his breath, swirling his finger rings around and around as he continues to grin widely as if he just hit the jackpot.

Wait, did he just say *her*? Fingering my sunglasses, I take them off, and run my fingers through my straight black hair to get the escaped strands out of my eyes. I quickly tie my shoulder length hair back on top of my head while looking around for said female. She must be something since she caught Tey's attention. He gets bored easily.

Casually leaning against the stone fireplace that takes up half the wall, I hear a click of heels on the marble flooring and the muttering of Logan's father as he rounds the corner with his wife right by his side. I used to know his first wife, she was like a mother to me, even more so than my own who is a stone cold, frigid bitch but I'm still not sure about his new wife. Their wedding happened so fast, it seemed like moments after his first wife, Helen, was lowered into the ground, and Logan has a hatred towards Diana that even has me wary. I'll back up my best friend, heck I'll even hide a body for him if he needs me too, but the way he's grown heartless like my own father keeps me on my toes, constantly in fear that we'll really lose him one day to this cruel world.

"Nicky, what are you doing here?" A shaking, Diana, reaches the couch and practically drops into the cushions with her face pale and withdrawn.

What is wrong with the Chief's wife now? God, she's dramatic.

Her normally straight blonde bob is sticking up in all angles, her eyes circled by dark shadows as if she hadn't slept, and the faraway look in her brown eyes has me glancing back and forth between her and Franco.

"I was asked to stop by, business," I answer with a shrug and don't say anything else because she doesn't know about the side business aspect... Well, I suspect she knows and she just turns a blind eye to it.

The way she ignores the crime part of our lifestyle has me always watching her more closely because only someone who grew up in a world full of violence wouldn't blink if a man was shot in front of you in cold blooded murder. It's hard to trust her and with reason, of course. If Logan asked me to help him dump her body into the ocean, I wouldn't even question the reason why. She wasn't around when we were kids and she's an outsider that may know too much already. Hell, my own father has killed men for less, turning your back on your enemies gets you killed and that's what happens when you couldn't care less if someone dies or not.

I look down at my knuckles, seeing the scars healed over and over from being reopened as the wooden cane snapped across my fingers for discipline at age eight. That was the year I started to understand how the world can stand still while pain seems to make you suffer in silence. I'm very skilled at how to torture someone, to get information out of them, and that's not only with the techniques I possess with the computer. I'm a hacker by heart, it's set in my bones, and you can't hide a single thing from me.

"Ah, the real fun is about to begin. Good morning, sugar plum! You are looking refreshed, nice shower?" Tey turns his head towards the stairs with a gleeful smirk and licks his wide lips at whoever he's staring at.

I pull my gaze away from his mouth, which seems to become harder and harder these days, and glance sharply towards the staircase at the sound of soft, padded feet coming down along with the pounding steps of a pissed off Logan. I'd recognize that sound anywhere, he's always moved in anger and it's gotten worse over the years, the more Franco assigned us jobs on the street that someone our age shouldn't be doing. My gaze lands on Logan first, seeing his eyes already hardened into a pissed off glare at the person in front of him. I follow his gaze and my heart skips a small beat before pounding in sync to match her footsteps. A chuckle sounds beside me but I'm hardly paying attention. Dark brown eyes are staring into mine, studying me as I hold perfectly still leaning against the mantel. I'm also afraid to move, the fear of scaring her away like a baby deer because she keeps glancing around like she's about to make a run for it.

Don't run, please for the love of God, don't run. Men like me and my brothers love a good chase, and who knows what would happen once she's caught. Deep inside I'm kind of hoping she bolts.

"Tey, shut your mouth for once in your life," Franco says in exasperation, leveling a hard look at the fool who only grins wider before Franco glances back at the girl. "Tillie, take a seat. This is going to be a lot for you to process and it's probably best if you're sitting down." Franco warns in a commanding voice to do as he says, gesturing to the couch opposite of his wife.

I think deep down he really does care for Diana, but something inside of him died when Helen was murdered and the fucking killer was never caught. That changes a man, makes him dead inside but there's still a spark for him to care for his new wife, as he treats her like fragile glass and maybe she is. Who knows? I still don't trust the bitch. She came off the streets basically, a hoe looking for money, and she trapped Franco with her looks and fake lies. Now she has it all; a big house, money at her disposal, and all she has to do is fuck Logan's father to keep him happy. A win/win for her.

"Listen, I'm thankful for you welcoming me into your home but maybe it was a mistake coming here. I'll show myself out the door," Tillie says in a soft whisper, having me straighten from the mantel and taking a step in her direction but Logan beats me to her.

He doesn't say a word, just grabs her elbow and steers her to the couch, releasing her as if her touch burned him before taking up a stance on the other side of the mantel from me. Very interesting. Who is this girl? Dressed in black leggings, a purple crop top that shows off her smooth stomach just below her belly button that I find oddly cute, and she's barefoot... Did she plan on leaving without anything else? What is going on? My arms ripple with the need to choke answers out of someone if they don't start talking. I cross my arms over my chest and see her glance at me out of the corner of her soulful eyes before I look away bored. I feel something spark in my chest that surprises me. I cut myself off from everyone except my tight knit group of friends, but just one look at her face tells it all to me.

Pain, lots of pain that never seems to go away, no matter how much you smile; it's sketched in deep lines around your eyes. I see it all and it makes me mad. I don't like feeling anything because if you can't feel anything then nothing can get to you. I'll just pretend she isn't here. Just another girl who means nothing.

I wonder why she was limping slightly before sitting down, and is that a dragon tattoo on her lower back?

"Why are you here?" Franco demands, pulling me out of my musings as he stares down at Tillie.

For some reason, the thought of him killing her doesn't sit well with me and I can see I'm not the only one as Tey finally sits up from the floor, looking tense. Logan doesn't fool me as he stares out the front windows, but I can see his trigger finger twitching. This is bad, very bad and I'm really glad Dalton isn't here. The man sees something he likes and just takes it without asking. He'd eat this girl up and spit her out without breaking a sweat. I could be wrong because the hard glint in this girl's eyes says a different story. She pushes her shoulders back and flickers her gaze over to a quiet Diana without looking away. My gaze swings back and forth. I'm missing something here.

"I was sent here. I was told that I'd be able to find someone to help me," she says, clenching her fist tight in her lap.

"Who told you that?" Diana finally speaks, her voice has a small tremble and she leans heavily against Franco.

"I told you already, Doris did. She didn't give me any details. Just shoved your address into my hand and told me to get away until I ended up here. How do you know her? Were you a sweetbutt too?" Tillie asks softly, her shoulders stiffening as Diana wavers on the couch.

"I-I don't know how this is possible. It can't be," Diana whispers under her breath and stands, making her way towards a stiff Tillie who eyes her warily.

She doesn't trust easily and is as fidgety as a rabbit as she leans away from Diana when she drops to her knees at her feet. I shoot Logan a look that asks what the hell is going on but he's staring down Tillie with an unreadable expression crossing his face.

"I wasn't a sweetbutt. I was an old lady." Diana's lip wobbles and she reaches her hand out to touch Tillie's face but she dodges away and scoots along the couch before she stands up quickly and jumps over the cushions to put as much distance between a distraught Diana and herself.

"Who's old lady?" Tillie asks, breathing heavily and her gaze looks faraway.

"Shit, Diana! I didn't know you were part of Hell's Devils! Dalton's gonna freak the fuck out when he finds out," Tey announces and stands up quietly, edging towards the front door to block Tillie's path in case she makes a run for it.

Everyone seems to freeze at the expression on her face as if she senses danger in the room... Only people who know what to look for, experienced the same thing in life, know that everyone in here is a killer.

"Who's Dalton?" Tillie asks frantically in a raspy voice, her eyes darting to Tey and flickering behind him for an escape exit.

She's going to make a run for it, I just know it. She looks like a scared, trapped cat in the back of an alley but I'm feeling like this kitten has claws. I'm going to easily catch her before she knows what happened. It's the thrill for me and I'm a junky.

"He's the Hell's Devils president's son. You'll meet him tomorrow when you start school, I won't tolerate not having an education in this household. You'll finish high school and catch up quickly even if it's the middle of the semester. Right?" Franco doesn't wait for her to respond, he won't take no for an answer. "I'm going to just get to the point because I have other important business to attend to," he mutters offhandedly, glancing down at his phone with his brow scrunched, distracted.

Whatever he has to say, I have a feeling it is going to turn this girl's world upside down. I study her closely, having the need to know everything about her and itching to get to my computer to see what I can dig up. She's a mystery to me, she looks afraid but has an air about her that she's flipping everyone the finger with a big fat fuck you.

"What is the point, Franco?" Logan asks impatiently,

looking like he wants to wrap his hands around his father's neck to get answers.

"Tillie, Diana is your mother and for now you'll be under my care until... we can get more answers." Franco stares down at a very pale Tillie, her arms wrapping around herself as she shakes her head back and forth.

Her wide brown, expressive eyes stare in shock, and the grip on her arm is bruising enough that it makes my own fist clench onto nothing. I don't like that she's hurting herself, I'd rather cause the pain for her if she needs it that badly.

"You're lying! My mom is Lorrie-" She cuts off at Diana's cry of dismay.

I sneer down at the pathetic woman balling her eyes out on the living room floor instead of trying to comfort her daughter. Tey shuffles on his feet, repeatedly glancing at Tillie while sucking on his lip ring. He hates the high emotions in here just like me but he hardly knows this girl and looks like he wants to pull her into his arms.

Tillie sways on her feet, her fingers digging into her elbows as she frantically looks around for a way out. Logan makes a frustrated noise in the back of his throat, glaring at his father who acts like drama isn't unfolding right in front of him. I say fuck it and push off the mantel to leap over the couch before this beautiful girl can notice I'm right beside her. Gently grasping her elbow, she glances up at me with lost, chocolate eyes and a shake of her head in dismay. I think of the best way to push myself when I'm lost in my own head and that's anger.

"So, this girl shows up out of the blue and suddenly she's part of the family? I don't know Franco... kind of convenient to me. What if she's a spy? Didn't we just have some shipment go missing? Timing seems off to me and I don't trust her." I stare down at her as I say this, seeing the tightening of her facial expression and her lip drawing in a stubborn pissed off line.

That's more like it, baby, give me all your anger. I can absorb it like a sponge, practically thirsty for it.

"I'm leaving. This was a mistake coming here. I'll disappear another way instead," she mumbles under her breath.

An interesting turn of events, I glance at Tey and Logan to see if they caught that mishap of hers. They did. Seems we are all on the same page. She's not going anywhere until we have some answers. She caught my attention.

"No. You'll be staying here," Franco commands, dismissing her as he bends forward to kiss Diana's forehead before turning towards Logan as he heads out of the room. "She's under your wing, don't let her out of your sight." He leaves after dropping that bomb with Logan chasing him out of the living room.

Ah, so he thinks the timing is off too. Looks like she's not going anywhere and for some crazy reason that excites me. Time to trap the little bird and claim some answers past her sweet lips.

"I wouldn't bother with any lies. We'll find out everything and there will be consequences if you stab us in the back." I threaten her, her jaw clenches as she yanks her elbow out of my grasp.

"Si-sit down, Til, and I'll explain everything, please," Diana begs, grimacing as she picks herself up off the floor and takes a seat on the couch, patting the spot next to her.

Tillie eyes her suspiciously but finally sits down with her back ramrod straight, completely uncomfortable. Nodding my head at Tey, he follows me so we can catch up with Logan and Franco. Crazy fucker is whistling under his breath and I can't help but roll my eyes at the excitement he has radiating off him in waves. Looks like we both won't be bored for a while.

Fuck. I wish I didn't feel this way. I'm annoyed with having her here. She's a distraction that I can't seem to pull my gaze away from. Her eyes tell you exactly what she's thinking.

Shaking my head, I step through the office door and lean against the bookcase that lines the room with a clear view of the whole space. Logan sits in the chair on the other side of his dad's desk while Tey strolls over to the floor to ceiling windows and gazes outside. I notice a small bulge in Tey's pocket and have to stifle a chuckle. My eyes must deceive me because that's not his dick, I would know, I stare enough as it is. He's carrying around that stuffed unicorn animal again. He's bounced around from house to house in all of L.A. but the one thing that's always been with him is that damn unicorn he found. I think it adds to his craziness and if anyone gives him shit about it, I'll silence them.

"Right. I'm getting straight to the point boys. I want eyes and ears on that girl, if my hunch is right we might not need to worry about anything. Nicky, I'm going to give you some names and tell me everything you can find on them." Franco leans back in his desk chair, steepling his hands together as he eyes us. "Have you heard of the Demon Jokers in Nevada?"

I suck in a sharp breath because no way in hell does that delicate flower have any relations with that motorcycle gang. If I had a daughter, she wouldn't even be in the same county as those lowlife backstabbers. In the underground crime world, you come to know who is who, and let's just say the President of that club is fucked up in the head. I've heard stories, brothers against brothers, the way they treat women and children reminds me of my own father. It's just not possible.

"What about them?" Logan asks, clenching the armrests on his chair even though his face is stoic.

"Tillie is owned by that club and until I know more, that she wasn't sent here as a spy or to cause chaos in my business, you four will be keeping a close eye on her at all times. From the moment she wakes up in the morning to when she goes to sleep, I mean it. Go buy her some clothes for tomorrow and don't fuck this up, boys." Franco glances at Logan meaningfully and shakes his head in exasperation when we hear a loud cry coming from the front of the house.

Without another word, he strides out of his office and leaves us deep in thought.

"Dalton is going to shit his pants. Shall we head over to his place to fill him in on the game we'll be playing with my pet?" Tey asks, rubbing his hands together before throwing an arm over my shoulder as we head out.

I usually live for the dull moments in my life, to find some inner peace in the chaos but I have a feeling that's all going to end and it's all because of the girl with brown eyes that penetrate my soul.

CHAPTER 9

Tillie

The silence is getting to me, I've been sitting in front of my *mother* for five solid minutes after the guys left the room. She keeps staring at me like I've risen from the grave and come to haunt her.

"So..." I start, squirming on the overly comfortable couch and darting my gaze towards the front door.

The nagging feeling that I've made a mistake coming here grows. I'm not afraid physically, but mentally I feel like I'm spiraling down a dark hole that I might not be able to climb out of. Cruz had hidden his true self behind a mask for a long time before his true colors came through but these guys don't hide anything. The aura of danger surrounds them, you can tell how their demeanor is with the way they hold themselves and the slightly crazed assholes enjoy it. Logan has been point blank with me, told me how it is, even if he's being an ass. The man may have big dick energy, which I can now confirm by the sore ache between my thighs but God, he's such an asshole! As for Tey... I can't really describe him, but oddly enough I find him sweet even if he carries a knife in his boot. And lastly, Nicky, who wouldn't stop glaring at me with his almond shaped emerald eyes. I felt burned to a crisp under his intense gaze. The guy confuses me, how deadly still he was but didn't miss a thing in the room. This whole experience has turned my normal routine upside down. I'm used to walking on my toes, waiting for the next beating but with these people, if they wanted me to be dead... I'd already be dead. It's just a gut feeling I've learned to follow over the years, you get used to the difference between seeing how a sociopath works or if that person is just damaged inside and out. That doesn't mean I'll be walking around without looking over my shoulder. The threat was loud and clear. I'm not trusted. I don't know what they think I did but I shouldn't be here in the first place. Diana clearing her throat causes me to jump, so lost in my thoughts, and focus back on her.

"You aren't supposed to be alive," she blurts out, patting down her fake blonde hair in a nervous gesture.

I don't- can't decide how to even answer that. My life has been a shit show, it wasn't the worst until after Uncle Rig disappeared. Did I ever think about what it would be like if I wasn't here anymore? To just be no more? Of course, I've been tempted to just take the easy way out but my life couldn't be just misery. The thought makes me angry... no, completely furious.

"And why the hell would you think that? You know nothing of my life and what I've been through. I'm a fucking survivor! This was a mistake, coming here." My chest was tight, making it difficult to breathe and I realized the symptoms I was having could only be one thing, an oncoming panic attack.

Everything was just too much. The thought of Lorrie really not being my birth mom... and this lady in front of me, who looks put together when her daughter was out there slowly dying each day, sends me over the edge. Not to mention I let my wings spread with my asshole of a step-brother. Will nothing really surprise me anymore? I don't give a shit about Franco's warning, I'm not a prisoner. Never again. As soon as I can breathe normally again, I'm out of here. My head was suddenly pushed between my knees. I inhaled deep breaths and noticed the quiet sob next to me that somewhat helped me focus on something else.

"That came out wrong. I'm sorry. I meant that I didn't know you were alive. It's a long story and I really want you to hear me out before you consider leaving, Til," Diana whispers brokenly, her hand smoothing up and down my back in an attempt to comfort me.

I jerk away from the small touch before she can feel my scars, and put some space between us. A soft whisper in the back of my mind tries to break through. An edge of dark-ness, I think it's the gentle touch that I've never received that brings the past trying to break free.

"W-what do you mean?" I stutter out, trying desperately to focus on anything that isn't broken in my mind.

"Eighteen years ago, I gave birth to a beautiful baby girl that stole my heart the moment she looked at me with big, brown eyes. I became a mama that day, but the only remaining piece of my heart broke then too." She pauses, her gaze faraway before focusing back on me with tears in her eyes. "I like to think you were sent to me when my life was so hopeless, a brightness in a place filled with such darkness..." Her voice trails off in a whisper, tears trailing down her face that looks so much like mine but older.

This is hard to wrap my head around. It was drilled into my head that Lorrie was my mom ever since I could remember. Even Uncle Rig would never deny who my mom was when I asked him a long time ago. I knew at a young age that she wasn't mother material when she would call me a worthless waste of space. I didn't know why she would treat me that way but it kind of makes sense now... I was never hers from the beginning.

"Uncle Rig, why does my mom hate me?" I asked around a mouthful of peanut butter and jelly as we sat outside on the picnic table.

Uncle Rig always seems to know when I'm starving, even comes to get me to go get ice cream sometimes. When I'm bigger than eight years old, old enough to make my own meals, I won't have to have anyone to look after me. I'll be a grown up, life will be easier. I guess Uncle Rig can stick around to get me ice cream sometimes too, I'll always need him.

"Your mother would never hate you. If she knew... she loves you with everything inside of her. One day, she'll show you if you just give her time. For now, you have me to love the shit out of ya, kid," Uncle Rig says, ruffling my hair, and laughing at my jelly filled grin.

"Why would you leave me to that monster if you knew I was there?" The small whisper leaves my mouth without thinking about it, my body shaking from the shock.

"Your birth was a difficult one. I didn't have nurses to help me, only the club's Doc as I gave birth to you on the pool table in the compound. Hours of struggling, bleeding, you finally appeared in my arms. I was exhausted, could barely keep my eyes open but I got to hold you for what felt like seconds. You gripped my finger with your tiny hands, so strong that I knew you would be okay. Everything was ripped away from me when Payne and Doc took you to be looked after. That night, Til, I was told you died from complications. I couldn't believe it, you were just in my arms and then you were gone. A piece of me died that night. I was so weak, tired, that I just became a shell of myself. Days passed and I never came out of my bedroom, wishing I was anywhere but there. It was too much and Payne carried on like he always did. I was as good as dead and that's when I left without a backwards glance." She reaches out to grip one of my hands tightly, her gaze flickering between mine, begging for me to understand.

"I still don't get it. Why would Payne tell you I was dead? He never wanted me there, he passed me around..." I trail off, lost in my memories, and nearly jump out of my skin when Diana cries out as if in pain.

Her shoulders are hunched, crying openly over our clasped hands as she rocks back and forth. Franco comes storming around the corner, his lips in a tight line as he wraps an arm around Diana, helping her off the couch.

"This has been a painful memory for my wife. You'll have to wait until she's feeling better. For now, feel free to explore the house and make yourself at home since you won't be going anywhere. You'll be under the boys' care and will be starting school tomorrow. I'll be making the calls to have you enrolled and everything else you might need." His tone comes off as polite but what he's really saying is that I'm a prisoner in his home until he figures out what to do with me.

I'm still free to come and go as I please, as long as one of the guys is watching me like a fucking babysitter. But the thing is, I'm not going anywhere until I have answers and it might just be a safer route for me... until it's not.

I hear the distant sound of vehicles purring to life outside, the sound never ceases to send a shiver down my spine. Guess the three of them left without another word. I stay planted on the couch, trying to process everything as I watch Diana leave the room, leaning against her husband for support. She really is fragile. She stops suddenly at the archway but doesn't turn around.

"He was punishing me," she whispers on a choked sob and leaves the room to probably go lay down again.

What was Payne punishing her for? He isn't even here but wins once again as he takes another piece of my life from me that I never knew existed.

CHAPTER 10

Tillie

*H*ave you ever watched a tornado, seen the way it moves in one direction then suddenly changes course all the while causing so much damage that nothing is left behind?

That's how my Monday morning is going.

I was beyond exhausted after my chat with my *mom* yesterday that I stayed mostly in my new room and only left for food, sneaking into the kitchen to raid the pantry like a freaking hermit. At some point leaving the room, I found shopping bags right outside my bedroom door full of new clothes that were all in my size. I don't know why or how but damn if it didn't feel good trying on something that isn't used. The whole ensemble is completely different, every article of clothing from top brand name places like Chanel to Gucci. From light pastels dresses to all dark and leather. I like it, it's different and fits my ever changing mood. I went to sleep last night in the bed, deciding that with the kitchen knife under my pillow, I'd be able to cut anyone before they got too close or so I thought.

The sunlight is shining through my curtains, demanding I open my eyes to start getting ready for my first day of a new school but that wasn't what really fully woke me up. I've always been a light sleeper, had to be, so it caught me by surprise when the warm body next to mine didn't wake me up sooner. It was the finger twirling in my hair that had my eyes snapping open in an instant. Before I know it, my knife is out from under the pillow and pressing against a strong, male throat as I breathe heavily on top of the intruder with my vision blurry around the edges. The deep, dark chuckle curls around me like a lover's caress and wakes me up like a shot of caffeine to my system.

"We really gotta stop meeting like this, sugarbutt. Well, maybe not, I kind of like it." Tey smiles wickedly underneath me, relaxing back into the bed as if I'm not about to cut his throat open.

"Jesus Christ! Do you have a death wish? This is way too early for me. I need coffee before I come face to face with your psycho ass," I mumble grumpily, not kidding about the coffee part.

Tey grins lazily up at me, crossing his arms behind his head and it's then that I notice I'm still in his lap and there is a hard bulge growing under my ass. I remove the knife from his skin and scrub a hand down my face. How the hell do they keep getting into my room? I even shoved a chair under the doorknob last night... which I see is now missing when I glance over at the door.

"Don't we all have a death wish? A way to go out on our own terms? This would be a beautiful way to go." His teeth flash before he moves and I suddenly find myself under him, his piercing blue eyes holding me in place as the breath is knocked out of me.

"You know, you have the prettiest eyes, kind of sad when you look closely but that doesn't mean I wouldn't put them in a jar to keep. Hey, how many kids do you want? I want at least ten if that's good with you? Oh, look at the time, sunshine! Time to get your delicious ass out of bed and ready for school." He chuckles at my shocked expression before bending down to nip at my neck, making my pulse jump wildly under the small touch.

I'm still laying in a daze, not sure what just happened but he's at the door suddenly, looking back at me with my messy bed head and breathing like I just went for a run. My brows draw together in confusion when he reaches into his jean pocket and pulls out a small stuffed unicorn.

"I'd be careful where you step, Tillie. Even the brightest things in this life dull after some time." He stares down at the stuffed animal with blond brows wrinkled together before flashing me a wink and leaving my room.

"What the ever loving fuck just happened?" I ask out loud and don't get a response, of course.

With a groan, I drag myself out of bed and make my way across the room towards the vanity table and see an outfit laid out for me. Did he just decide my clothes for the day? I mean he has good taste, he picked out something that fits my mood perfectly this morning. Anxiety is riding me hard today, the thought of going to a new school and I'm terrified that if I step outside in the daylight that Cruz will show up out of nowhere and steal me back to hell. I know that I've put miles between him and me, but it still makes my heart pound and my palms sweaty.

Staring at my drained reflection in the mirror of the vanity, I lean forward to look myself in the eye.

You're a bad bitch and you fucking got this.

Does the pep talk help? Sure, but does it make the fear go away? Hell no! But it does get me moving to start getting ready.

Throwing off my sleep shorts and tank top, I pick up the red thong that goes great against my tan skin and can't help the giggle that leaves my mouth. Tey really is too much but what he doesn't know is that I live for the scandalous lingerie to give me a boost of confidence. Slipping them on with the matching bra, I shimmy my hips into a pair of black ripped, skinny jeans and a black tank top that hugs the girls for support. Brushing out my hair that has an edge of dark purple, I slip it into a high ponytail, and coat my lips in gloss, calling it a day. My reflection shows a girl who is makeup free, natural tan skin glowing, and bright brown eyes with long lashes. I can be me without having to hide behind a mask anymore. It's all I ever wanted and I'll be damned if I have to take a step back when I could be running forward instead.

With a grin, I swipe my new expensive leather jacket off the dresser, it slips through my arms like butter, and I slip my feet into my black docs. Perfect. I'm ready to be the new me and it feels good. My stomach is still tied up in knots but I've been through worse than high school. Only six more months and I'll be done, to do whatever I want, finally free. I swing the door open and am not looking where I'm going as I grumble under my breath about needing to stop hiding when I slam into a brick wall. The brick wall that just so happens to be Logan's firm chest. Biting my lip, I peek up at him from under my lashes to see his nostrils flaring and his honeyed eyes glaring down at me.

"Don't have all day to wait on you, baby girl. We leave in

five so hurry your ass up," he growls and practically shoves me out of the way causing me to stumble over my own feet.

You know that pep talk about starting new and not taking any shit. It starts right the fuck now.

"Whatever you say, dearest brother," I say sickly sweet while fluttering my lashes. He whips around with narrowed eyes and before I know what's happening, his hand is pulling on my ponytail, and he slams his lips down on mine in a punishing, harsh kiss. I swear I taste blood in my mouth from when our teeth clashed together. Why does this send a thrill through me? It's hard and demanding but oddly gentle from his big hand sliding slowly down my spine to grip my ass cheek.

"That's stepbrother to you. Know your place, Tillie." His voice is husky and forceful but the growing evidence against my hip tells me all I need to know.

"And where is my place?" I ask, narrowing my eyes up at him when he smirks, a dimple appearing in his cheek.

"On your knees," he says darkly and pushes me away which causes me to trip over my feet once again and I catch myself at the last second before landing on my ass.

Grinding my teeth together, I watch his broad shoulders disappear down the stairs and curse at how my stomach flutters.

"We'll see who ends up on their knees," I whisper.

The white BMW i8 vibrates under my ass and it takes everything inside of me to not moan, my nails digging into my thighs but I don't think it escapes Tey's notice as he twirls a lock of my hair from the seat behind me with a chuckle. Why did they make me sit in the passenger seat? It's as if they knew this car would have me drooling and my panties soaked. I can't help it, it's in my blood to appreciate things that are worthy and this car is... *the* perfect racing car. Wonder if I could sneak it out sometime for a ride without Logan finding out?

Twenty minutes of pure torture and I'm almost happy when we reach the school parking lot. A Ducati Panigale V4 motorcycle pulls in right beside us, nearly making my eyes pop out of my head. My fingers twitch to get out and steal that bike for a joy ride because those babies are fast, real fucking fast. The rider looks directly at me through the tinted window before sliding off his helmet. I should have guessed it was Nicky. Grey dress pants mold to his muscular thighs as he swings his legs over the seat and a white button down does wonders for his arms with his sleeves rolled up. Two words: arm porn. Colorful sleeve tattoos cover both of his arms, and I want to get closer to discover every inked inch of him. Nicky walks to the front of the car and waits, he almost looks bored but I can see the watchful way he glances around. Seeing the population of high school kids, talking to friends, on their phones, and dressed in designer clothes... it all makes me feel like I belong in the trash because I don't fit in here. Welcome to Beverly Hills High, where the rich and famous flash money like it's nothing. Logan clears his throat as he turns off the car, twisting in his seat to look me over before glancing at Tey with a raised brow.

"Dalton is waiting for you in classroom 315 to give you the grand tour. Stay out of the spotlight, don't get in our way, and be a good girl." Logan smirks like the ass he is and climbs out of the car without another glance back at me as he makes his way across the packed parking lot.

Damn him. Heads turn as he walks by, guys nodding in

that weird way but eye him cautiously at the same time. Girls adjust their already short tops so they lay a little lower and flutter their fake lashes. Fake tans, bottle hair dye, and high heels pretty much describe the girls in a California high school. Logan is surrounded in seconds with an easy grin and throwing an arm over some blonde, big breasted chick. Jealousy flares in my stomach, catching me off guard because I've never, ever had this feeling for a guy before. At least Nicky just walks by his friend's side, all cool and collected, pushing away any girl that slides up to him. Why do I care? I don't know or own these guys. They're all assholes.

"There, there, little dove, don't take it so personally. Lo jumps from girl to girl. Let's get you inside because I have shit to do," Tey says, hopping out and opening the door for me while pulling a joint from his pocket and lighting up without a care in the world.

Guess the rules don't apply to these guys.

I take a deep breath and follow a high Tey towards the school double doors, ignoring the curious glances shooting our way. If looks could kill, I'd be dead a hundred times over by now. Way too many girls are glaring at me as if I stole their favorite lipstick. I straighten my spine and walk with my head held high, I don't owe these people anything.

I almost lose Tey in the crowd of teenagers hanging by their lockers, shuffling in the tight hallways towards their morning classes before the bell rings. I hate the stares, the leer from the guys as I move along with the student body. It feels like walls are closing in around me as the panic starts to set in. Loud male laughter rings out as my gaze flickers around, drawing my attention to a group of jocks at the end of the hall surrounding a locker. Three sets of male eyes are on me, like a pack of animals at a watering hole. One in particular jock with red hair in a jersey slides his slimy brown gaze up and down my body with a cocky grin. Tall, muscular, and a guy who thinks women belong on their knees, a typical school bully jock. I know men like him ooze confidence because they think a woman will never say no to them, I'm the new meat in their territory.

Shit.

A muscular chest and broad shoulders covered in a soft cotton black t-shirt blocks the jocks' view as a wave of dizziness comes over me. A single finger tilts my chin up, making me look into arctic ocean eyes.

"It's a playground of wild, horny animals. Vicious and deadly. Welcome to Beverly Hills High," Tey mutters with a lazy grin, his bright blonde hair falling over his eyes, hiding that all too knowing gaze from me.

"You're really fucking crazy aren't you?" I eye him with a raised brow, seeing so much he tries to hide behind the weed, the loneliness.

I don't think anyone really knows the real Tey and lucky me is seeing his true colors that are hidden behind a mask I want to peel off his perfect face.

"Only the craziest, baby," he whispers so only I can hear and leans forward, skimming his nose along my neck with a deep inhale before stepping back. "See you later, starfish. Room 315. Dalton has your schedule." He turns away, leaving me to find the fucking class alone and the Hell's Devils son, aka Dalton.

Without him invading my space, it's like a bubble popped and the noise returns. The mutters and bangs of lockers almost make me jump, forgetting for a second that we were standing in the middle of the crowded hall while classmates walk by staring. I shake my head at his retreating back and the silliness of the nicknames he's been using for me. I kind of like them. They're not as annoying and I look forward to seeing what other ridiculous nicknames he will come up with.

Glancing around, I swear under my breath, noticing every goddamn person is gawking at me like I'm a freaking leper. A lanky, nerdy guy with a Star Wars shirt hanging loose on him, walks by with his head down as he clenches his bookbag strap in a death grip and pushes his glasses up his nose.

Perfect. I don't need another towering, all ripped muscles jerk over my shoulder, and he looks nice enough.

"Hey!" He jumps at my overly excited outburst and jerks his head up, looking behind him left and right to see if I'm talking to him.

"Me?" He asks softly, all shy, his hazel eyes big behind his glasses.

"Yeah, you. Do you mind pointing me in the direction of room 315?" I ask, pulling him out of the way by the strap of his bag as one of those ass jocks walk by, about to bump into him.

"Watch where you're going freak." The douche jock sneers, both of us choosing to ignore him.

"S-sure, it's uh, on the second floor. I'll um, walk you there if you'd like?" I actually find his blush adorable and the slight stutter.

I just really want to hug the guy, which by the way, I'm not a hugger of any type but he feels safe. He doesn't look like he wants anything from me but maybe friendship. He hasn't once stepped into my space or looked at my body.

Dear God, is it possible for me to have a male friend?

"That would be great! I'm Tillie." I smile softly, just staring directly at him and raise an eyebrow as he continues to stand there, pushing those big glasses up his nose nervously.

"Oh, yeah, I'm Evan. Let's go before I'm uh, late for physics." He practically squeaks and turns on his converse in the opposite direction.

I follow by his side, noticing how empty the halls are becoming, and dreading the whole new girl act. I'll cut someone if they make me stand in front of the class to tell my life story. I don't care if I'm starting in the middle of the school quarter, my story is my own.

"Listen, you might not want to be caught walking with me again unless you want to be thrown in a locker, a toilet swirl, or tossed into the dumpster after school. Here's the class, it was nice, um, meeting you," he says nervously, looking away in embarrassment until he notices that I haven't said a thing, and glances back at me with a confused expression.

The hallways are clear of moving bodies as we stand outside of the closed door of classroom 315. I'm about to do something scary, so unlike me, that it catches me off guard. Quicker than he can react, I grab his shoulders and hug him like a favorite stuffed animal. His surprised squeak makes me giggle and I know I've hit my limit when my body stiffens as a memory tries to break through. I release him and keep my hands on his shoulders so he looks me in the eye.

"We're going to be the best of friends. Thank you for being so kind, and I'll look for you at lunch so we can see what classes we have together. Save me a seat." His mouth drops open and I have to bite my lip to hold my laughter inside.

He stands there, nodding his head like a bobblehead and I have to turn him around, giving him a small push to get him moving. Shaking my head once he's gone, I face the classroom, my nails biting into my fist because I'm not sure how I'm going to react with another biker from a different club on the other side of this door.

With a deep breath, I grab the handle and throw the door open before I lose my nerve but stop cold at what greets my eyes. My body won't move, I'm half in the doorway staring at the big muscled giant. Dalton, I'm assuming. He looks like the cocky type. I swear the guy is at least seven feet tall, twinkling violet eyes staring unblinking into mine as he leans back against the teacher's desk. Black hair shaved on the side but longer hair slicked back on the top of his head, his skin a beautiful, rich, light brown that makes his eyes hypnotizing. Everything about this guy is broad, big, and I'm pretty sure his muscles have muscles that make his black shirt and leather cut mold to his barrel chest. It's the slow lopsided smile spreading across his face that makes my eyes narrow. The woman between his legs stopped me for a second but if he thought this sight would scare me away or shock me, he's completely wrong. Not even when he makes the older woman, who has to be the teacher, keep bobbing her head. What is with these guys who think they can walk all over me, control me with the power they obviously have over everyone else but me?

Challenge accepted fucker.

Stepping into the room, I slam the door shut behind me loudly, trying not to smile as the woman jumps and is about to turn around but his big hand holds her in place on the back of her neck. If this is Dalton, I'm not impressed, time to show these asses that a girl who's been through things worse than death can rise from the ashes. I stalk forward on quiet feet without showing any emotions on my face.

Game on.

CHAPTER 11

Dalton

*M*y eyes keep flickering towards the door, growing impatient as the seconds tick by. Where the hell is this bitch? At least I have the eager redhead between my legs, slurping around my cock like a hoover vacuum cleaner while making these loud but annoying porn moans. Mrs. Sullivan has been after me for months, the thirty year old history teacher always wearing skin tight skirts and blouses with a few buttons undone each time I walk into her classroom. The coy glances, the little touches, and small smiles that are thrown my way were all the cues I needed to get her on her knees. Not really my type but the woman acts like she is in heat, wanting to feel younger by being with a younger guy. I saw this opportunity as a perfect time to shock the bitch. When the guys came racing into the club last night with news of a little guest at the most suspicious timing, we decided to keep her in line by making sure she knows who's in charge. I was game without even meeting her, no one messes with my family.

I'm a biker, born into this life with a loud fucking cry right out of the womb that even had the doctor scared to smack my ass. I've shown my loyalty plenty of times with blood for Hell's Devils. My best friends may not be part of the club but they've had my back since we were kids. Hell, they've helped me bury a body or two without any questions, that's what family does for you. Knowing that this Tillie chick is from the fucking Demon Jokers club, makes me blind with rage. Those scums have no morals, rules go flying out the window with our rivals. I may be a criminal but that doesn't mean I don't have a code to follow. The plan with the bitch is to make her every living moment miserable, to get her to confess why she's here. I swear if she's here to spy on us, I'll choke her, and dump her in acid so that no one can ever find her.

I glance at the clock above Mrs. Sullivan's desk, wondering where the hell this little girl is. I know Logan said he'd send her my way to scare the shit out of her but I wanna have my fun first. Nothing like intimidating the girl with something shocking and scandalous. Just the thought of playing a game with the rival gets my cock harder than steel and this slut on her knees thinks it's all for her but the excitement starts in my balls when the door handle starts to twist.

About damn time. I can't hide my grin even though it starts to slip away when the breath is knocked out of me. This is Tillie? Fucking hell, I'm in trouble. I'm going to murder those three for not giving me a warning. Now I understand the grumpy mood Logan is in, the way Nicky is more quiet than usual, and Tey's twinkle in his eyes.

She's standing in the doorway with plump parted lips as

she takes in the scene. Those sexy lips make me even harder than the slut with her mouth around my dick. All smooth gold skin, big brown expressive eyes that seem to speak for themselves. Man, if looks could kill... I stare at the curves on her body, not realizing I'm gripping Mrs. Sullivan's head to pull her deeper onto me even though she resists. I'm tempted to fling her away and prowl over to this gorgeous goddess but her narrowing eyes stops me, reminding me that she's the enemy. She slams the door hard, making the teacher choke on my dick in shock, not realizing that someone else is in the room with us. My hand slides to the back of her neck, holding her in place, she knows better than to question me. You want my cock then you follow my rules. She made her bed, so if she gets caught, that's on her.

"Kind of busy here, little bitch, I'll be with you in a bit. Keep sucking, Mrs. Sullivan." I smile widely at Tillie, my insides lighting up at the hard glint overcoming her gaze, her jaw tight when she doesn't look away.

The slurping sound of my dick getting sucked is loud, I'm anticipating her being disgusted and upset at the blowjob I'm receiving from my teacher. Nothing like making someone cower and under your control by bringing out their weakness.

Instead, none of that happens.

She cocks her head to the side, watching my dick being half sucked and it's a shame because most women can't fit my whole cock in their mouth. It's a blessing and curse being well endowed. Her dark brown and purple hair swings in her ponytail as she walks over to my side without giving away what she's thinking. Stopping next to me, she bites her lush bottom lip, making me almost groan out loud. She peers up at me from under her long, dark lashes, she stares at me for a hot second, and then faster than I can follow, she grabs Mrs. Sullivan's hair and shoves her down on my cock until she starts gagging and choking. My mouth parts on a deep inhale, never breaking her gaze and I already know I've lost today when her lips start to spread in a leisurely smile.

"If you're going to put it in your mouth, at least do it right," she says to Mrs. Sullivan, not looking at her once, and ignoring the teacher gagging loudly between my legs.

I hardly feel the mouth around me anymore, all my focus is right on the vixen by my side and I don't think my dick has ever been this hard. Believe me, growing up in a motorcycle club, there's been plenty of pussy on hand, but never someone who would dare challenge me.

My abs ripple as I feel all sorts of shit in my gut. She pulls Mrs. Sullivan's head back, letting her think she has time to breathe before pushing her back down on me in an instant. My nostrils flare, my cock weeping but not for the one choking on me. It's all for this little bitch in control.

"You're close aren't you?" She breaks eye contact to glance down at my thick cock trying to stuff its way down a gagging mouth, her breathing picks up so I at least know I'm not the only one affected.

I shift my hands to grip the desk behind me in a death grip, resisting the urge to grab her tight little body and fuck the daylights out of her. This isn't my game anymore, I can hardly think straight at the moment. She hesitantly reaches out to me, making me wonder why she's so cautious of touching me but that all flies out the window the moment she places her fingers on my body. So lightly, her delicate fingers glide across my stomach, her touch barely there with my shirt and cut in the way but it burns a trail down the ridges of my stomach. She smells of warm vanilla and it draws me closer but my gaze is caught on those fingers heading lower. A small laugh from her has my head snapping up to see her staring at me already and she quickly skips backwards, letting go of me and Mrs. Sullivan. The stupid teacher is gasping for air on the floor but I hardly look at her, standing up straight to follow this goddess with my dick hanging out and swaying for all to see.

"Well it's been lovely getting to know you Dalton but oh, look at the time. Have to get to class. If this is how the teachers treat their students, I can't wait to see what's in store for me." She smirks like she won the jackpot, already pushing through the door and holding up a piece of paper, confusing the hell out of me what she's talking about.

It clicks a second later and I'm trying to tuck myself back in my pants while swearing up a storm. She stole her class schedule out of my front pocket as I was distracted by her touch and thinking with my cock.

"Get back here you little bitch and get me off!" I shout in a grumbly, hoarse voice, tilting my head as she runs out of the class before I can stop her, her ass bouncing with every step.

"Until next time, biker." She chuckles lightly, practically skipping down the hallway, and disappearing down the flight of stairs.

I run my hands through my hair in frustration at how she got the drop on me and left my cock rock hard. Dropping my hands, I look over my shoulder at the scrambling teacher with makeup running down her face and her eager, greedy hands reaching for me. My deep chuckle stops Mrs. Sullivan in her tracks and she stares at me in confusion as I wipe tears of laughter off my face.

Fuck, the little bitch got me good and it makes me want to play another round with her. I adjust my pants before leaving the classroom, ignoring my name being called behind me, and pull out my phone to send a group text.

"Time to step up our game."

I leave it at that, pretending my phone isn't blowing up and wonder if I have enough time to beat one out in the bathroom with a certain vixen on my mind. Straightening my Hell's Devils cut, the hallways are empty, and decide yeah, I got time.

By lunch, I'm practically shoving people out of my way to get to the cafeteria. If pops saw the way I was acting, he'd slap me upside the head while disapproving. Nothing is supposed to matter but the club. Hell's Devils always come first, no time for chasing tail, and I have to be the best at everything if I'm going to take over one day in his place. I've pushed myself the hardest to achieve everything I've set my mind to, and right now it's on the woman with mouthwatering curves and an ass that could bring men to their knees. I've been hearing rumors all day about her, some I've even spread myself. The one I heard in third period almost made me choke on my own saliva, how Tey was hugging her in the middle of the hallway and letting her pet him.

I got a kick out of that one because no one touches Tey, and I mean *no one*. Sometimes he freezes up if we get too close to him unless he's high as a kite. My brother has been through some shit, still fighting his demons but a small slip of a girl just breezes by and suddenly he's calling dibs. Having to place the student body in a different direction for my own selfish reasons, I started spreading the word in third period and by now everyone knows she's open game. A target on her back until she comes crying and gives us what we demand from her. She's supposed to be sneered down upon while the school we rule treats her like garbage, making her feel alone. But she's still our property, so no one will go too far without our word of approval.

Usually, I'd skip the whole cafeteria scene but today I'll make an exception, it's not like I'm borderline obsessed or anything. I just can't pass up a direct challenge, it's part of who I am. Going through the double doors, I immediately see Nicky staring down at a table full of people without saying a word, and watch them all scramble to get out of his way. Always cracks me up that he doesn't even have to speak to cause people to go running while fearing for their lives. Comes in handy.

I crash into the chair next to him, smirking as he props his feet on the table and leans back with his arms crossed over his chest, closing his eyes. He's not fooling anyone, he's watching everything in the room and listening.

"You're just as bad as Tey. At least Logan understands that the girl doesn't belong," Nicky mumbles softly under his breath, peeking an eye open to look at me like I've lost my mind. "Nothing good ever comes our way and it's too convenient that right after a drug bust and missing money she shows up. I'll get the answers out of her, I for one suggest blackmail to get there."

What blackmail? We hardly know her but I'm willing to seek the answers out of her by any means necessary. Nicky probably has something on her already, his hacker computer skills sometimes scare me. If he wasn't my friend, I'd probably try to kill him with the knowledge he has on everyone in power. It's one of the reasons Logan's dad has so many people in his pockets, Nicky loves his blackmail.

"Hey fuckers, I think we should show my angel what kind of people she's staying with starting tonight," Tey whispers in my ear over my shoulder, almost making me shit my pants.

I hate when he does that, I didn't even hear him come up behind me. Why is he here? He's usually under the bleachers out on the field lighting up. I'm about to ask why the sudden appearance when I see him glaring at something across the room. You know it's bad when he pats his unicorn in his pocket to make sure it's still in there. Whatever he's plotting can't be good.

That brings a grin to my face until my gaze follows his, seeing what he's staring at. My hands form a fist on the table, and a possessive urge comes over me in waves. Tillie just walked in, her gaze sweeping over the cafeteria, stopping on us for a hot second but that's not what has me seeing red. It's when she suddenly smiles, her shoulders dropping in relief as she spots something in the back of the room and starts waving. I swear all three of our heads move as one as we see that nerd- can't remember his name- waving frantically at her.

"What's that, unicorn? Kill Evan until his blood is soaking into my shoes," Tey says quietly behind me, most likely whispering to his stuffed animal but I can't take my murderous eyes off that kid whose name is apparently Evan.

"Calm yourself, Tey. Looks like the girl is about to get a wake up call," Nicky says with a smile in his voice, my head whipping around to see Logan behind Tillie with his obsessed stalker wrapped around his arm.

Paris Hardley, the school's barbie popular girl, her daddy is a judge and known for letting criminals go free even when proven guilty. Paris has had a lady boner for Logan since freshman year and my stupid friend fucked her on one mistaken drunken night at a party. She's been following him around like a puppy since then, putting other girls in their place if they even think of side eyeing Logan. She still comes around even when Logan fucks girls behind her back or in front of her. She's ugly on the inside and outside, her face covered in thick coats of makeup. I'm still not sure why Logan hasn't thrown her to the curb, always letting her get away with shit most people wouldn't.

"Well, this is about to get interesting," I mutter, all of us watching Paris as she slides her gaze back and forth between Logan and Tillie. She hasn't stopped staring at the back of Tillie's head with a menacing glare. I don't like that.

Paris steps away from Logan and walks towards Tillie with a sneer, her one hand holds a drink and is suddenly pouring it over Tillie's dark, shiny locks. This makes me frown, what a shame, I like her hair. I bet it would look better around my fist.

As soda drenches her whole head and slides down her shoulder, she freezes on the spot with her hand dropping down to her side that she was waving towards Evan. I expect her to shriek with outrage, throwing a fit but I should have already known better. Her face stays stoic as she slowly pivots around on her heels and stares up at Paris who is an inch taller than her but I don't see any fear from her side profile. I swear you could hear a penny drop, that's how quiet the whole cafeteria has become, everyone holding their breath to see what the new girl will do. She leans to the side to glance at Logan, who just stands there with his arms crossed, smirking.

"Really? If you want to get me wet, you'll have to try harder than that. It's called foreplay, honey," she says sweetly, ignoring the murderous gaze Logan stares down at her as she shrugs off her leather jacket and flings it at a surprised Paris's face.

Now her screaming is expected and I watch with rapt

attention as Tillie turns with her head held high and walks over to that Evan kid, sitting down with her hair drenched as if nothing just happened.

"Man, I liked that jacket on her," Tey grumbles out, pouting.

I can't help but agree. It looked good on her.

"I already ordered her another one," Nicky says quietly, surprising me.

Before I can question him, he leans back in his seat again and closes his eyes. I meet Logan's gaze from across the room and he motions his head for me to follow him as he strides out of the cafeteria without another backwards glance at a still screaming Paris.

"Let's get the fuck out of here. Logan will want to plan for tonight," I say, jumping up and slapping Nicky on his back as I pass him to get him moving.

Striding out of the double doors, Tey throws his arm over Nicky, talking excitedly but doesn't notice how Nicky stiffens with the one simple touch before relaxing. I roll my eyes, wondering when they will just get it out of the way and make out already. The sexual tension gets to me at times and I'm not even remotely bi. I love pussy but damn.

Glancing one more time over my shoulder, I meet vicious, glaring brown eyes and she flips me off, turning to talk to the nerd. She just fucking dismissed me.

CHAPTER 12

Tillie

When you think my day can't get any more horrible than it already is, how wrong I am. At least I have a friend by my side to help me not panic and lose my shit. Evan may not know it but he's a life saver, if not for him, I would have lost it in the middle of the cafeteria in front of everyone. Showing my weakness in front of those assholes would have made everything else worse but the moment I sat down across from my new bestie, he didn't say a thing as he continued to eat his pizza. Just passed me napkins and asked if it was diet coke or not. My shoulders relaxed little by little, finding it kind of funny that it wasn't the worst thing that's happened to me and I loved the guy for making a joke out of it. And for the record, it was diet coke. That bitch.

The rest of the day passed by pretty quietly, besides the stares and shoves in the hallways, no one bothered me. None of my classes had the guys in it, and I count my blessings because I didn't like the way I felt around them. It felt like my skin was on fire, burning hotter and hotter each time I caught glimpses of them throughout the day though. I know it's something I'm not used to... lust. I was attracted to Cruz back in the day with a little crush, thought he was my whole world, someone to love me but not once did he make my heart pound in excitement and fear at the same time. He didn't make my panties wet with just one heated look.

My last class was gym. I was tempted to use the showers but by the nasty looks I kept getting in the locker room... it was best if I waited until I can make sure no one would try to steal my clothes or some pathetic drama shit, even if my hair was sticky and gross. I sat on the bleachers due to not having a gym uniform and it gave me a chance to look at the rest of the students. I was used to seeing people with money, being near Las Vegas gave me that experience of seeing money thrown away, but here it's very different. My old school was dirt poor with being on the outskirts of the city, so I'm not used to seeing cell phones out in the middle of class and girls in high heels like they came out of the womb running in Louboutins.

My gaze skirts over the group of girls with short shorts, rolling my eyes as they twirl their hair and flirt with the guys across the gym, giggling and batting their lashes. It was disgusting. I'll never be the girl who flirts and giggles, I'm more straight to the point because you might not have a tomorrow. That reminder makes me shift uncomfortably on the bleachers, the dull ache between my legs throbbing. I shouldn't have had sex with Logan, my apparent step-brother of all things, but it felt so good. Still don't trust the fucker even if he made me feel things that I thought were impossible. It's absolutely ridiculous that after years of feeling nothing, scared to hope and dream that the past wouldn't rule over me, I'm attracted to four men that I hardly know.

"Wat-watch out. Out. Out!" A girly high pitched scream comes from somewhere behind me and I instantly duck my head.

A basketball bounces off the bleacher higher up behind me, right where my head would have been. Straightening, I glance to the court, seeing Paris smiling with a lip curl at me as she pats a guy's arm lovingly, one of the jocks from earlier.

"Bitch. Bitch. Bitch!" The same voice that gave me warning from before shouts repeatedly and I turn around to see a girl with bright pink hair in a pixie cut flipping off Paris, not even looking at her.

Decked out in multiple colored neon tights, a deep purple tulle skirt, and a white shirt with Hello Kitty on the front, she buries her face back in the book she's reading which looks like a romance from here. She peaks over the pages, her almond shaped lime green eyes meeting mine for a split second before she ducks her head and goes back to reading her book. I'm about to get up to go sit next to her because why wouldn't I? She looks like a real person instead of someone fake, plus I love the style she has going on, but the gym teacher blows his whistle, dismissing class just as I start to stand. She bounces out of her seat quickly, her pink Jimmy Choo sneakers flashing as she runs down the steps and rushes across the gym to the exit but not before she chucks her book over her shoulder in a jerky movement without looking behind her like she had no control over her arm and letting out a small shriek at the same time.

It smacks Paris in the face, her screaming louder than the one who threw it. Justice served in my opinion. I'm determined to be that girl's friend, she might just be my hero dressed in Hello Kitty.

Sticking as close as I can to the walls, I'm rushing out of the gym and trying to reach the front of the school without running into anyone in the crowded halls. I can breathe easier once I'm outside, having a chance to glance around and groaning in misery when I see the guys surrounding Logan's car with a group of girls hanging all over them, except for Nicky but they do try to get his attention.

Well, this is fucking fantastic. I'm going to have to bull-doze my way through the fan club if I want a ride back to the temporary house. Glancing around desperately, I see Evan heading towards a bright red Jeep Wrangler in the back of the parking lot. Not thinking about it, I start chasing after him, very aware of the stares as I jog with my bag clutched to my chest and the humid air making my shirt stick to my back.

"Evan!" I pant behind him, shoving a purple strand of hair out of my eyes.

He spins around startled and darts his gaze around nervously before settling on me, a slight smile turning at the corner of his mouth.

"Hey, Till. Shit. I'm sorry! I didn't even think, just gave you a nickname like we've been friends for years instead of just a day." His eyes widen behind his glasses, a panicked look moving over his expression. "I mean, uh, if you know... if you want to be friends. No pressure," he gushes out on a deep inhale, running his hand through his thick curls on top of his head.

I can only stare at him, biting my lip as a laugh climbs up my throat. A loud engine roars in the parking lot some-where near the front of the school. Clearly, the owner needs attention because the person keeps pressing on the gas, drawing the noise out. I don't bother to look, I can feel his stare burning into my back. I quicken my pace with Evan until we're standing at his front bumper.

"That had to be the cutest thing I've ever seen. Yeah, you dork, we're friends." I clear my throat to contain my laugh, punching him on the shoulder and pretending to not notice when he winces at the small love tap. "Would you mind giving me a ride to my, um, house?"

He glances out of the corner of his eye towards the asshat who presses on the gas again, only louder this time, and I swear Evan's eyes couldn't get any bigger at whatever he sees. I blow out an annoyed breath fed up with the games. I'm about to turn around until Evan grabs my cheeks, squeezing my face so that my lips pucker out like a fish.

"Don't look. If you don't move, maybe they won't see us," Evan whispers out of the side of his mouth, it hardly looks like he's breathing.

I would laugh but it gets stuck in my throat as we hear multiple car doors slam shut, I wince at the sound. That poor car.

"Oh, God, they're coming this way! It didn't work! Screw it, get in the car!" Evan lets go of my face like I burned him, his expression horrified when he realized he was squishing my cheeks and touching me.

"Tillie!" Logan shouts, anger clear in his voice and that's my cue to leave.

I shove Evan towards the driver's side to get him moving and hurriedly dash around the front towards the passenger seat. We're both slamming the doors shut, tires squealing as he pulls out of his parking spot. My gaze unwillingly glances out of the side window as we roll by. Logan and Nicky stand a few feet away with identical clenched jaws. Mad as hell honey eyes glare into my window and quickly shifts to Evan like he just signed his death warrant.

Shit. I didn't think about this beforehand and now I've put Evan in the middle of it with a target on his back. I'm not supposed to leave their sides without one of them watching my every move but I need a moment to myself. My emotions swirling out of control after the day I've had, trying to drown me, and I refuse to let anyone see me this way. My gaze flickers to Nicky for a hot second just before we leave the school behind, my throat closing at the look of red-hot hatred in his emerald eyes.

At least Tey looks amused as he laughs his ass off, pointing at the jeep with that unicorn next to a huge motorcycle. That beast must be Dalton's, it has motorcycle club written all over it with the all black, shiny body and long handlebars.

"Should we just keep driving and never look back?" Evan asks jokingly, but by the uneasy way he keeps glancing out his side mirror, I think he's serious. "So, where to?"

"You know where Logan lives?" Speak of the devil.

I glance out of my side mirror, seeing a fabulous sports car racing right behind us and a pissed off owner inches away from Evan's bumper. It's strange that I hate Logan but don't at the same time. Growing up around criminals my whole life, I've seen true evil so it shouldn't come as a surprise that I end up running right back into them head-first. It's different though. These guys are dangerous, psycho, and possessive but I don't see empty stares that are void of any emotion. Each time I look directly at them, something is sparked alive in their gaze. Either with anger, violence, or lust. It scares me and yet gives me a rush I've been longing for. So it doesn't bother me that Logan is chasing after me, probably thinking of a way to punish me but little does he know I'm looking forward to it. Maybe it's because the fucker had his cock shoved so far up inside me that I saw stars I never thought I'd reach. I may have a love/hate relationship going on with him, but he gave me a piece of what living can feel like. My body tingles, raw desire shivering down my spine. I want more, to live until I've had it all. He doesn't even know what he started.

"Yeah, everyone knows where the princes live. They throw epic parties, not that I've ever been. I just hear the rumors." Evan starts to sweat, I can't tell if it's because of the humid air or the devil hot on our tails.

"Sweet. I'm staying there, so you can just drop me off at the gate." The jeep swerves before jerking back into our lane.

"I, uh, what? Yo-you live with him?!" He practically shouts and curses when he jerks the wheel to the right to avoid Logan as he whips out from behind us and cuts us off.

I watch him speed away in heavy Los Angeles traffic as I grab the oh shit bar and know he isn't going far so he can still keep an eye on me.

"Unfortunately. He's my stepbrother." Leaving it at that, I don't go into detail.

I let people think what they will. I learned a long time ago when someone has made up their mind, they won't hear a damn thing you're saying. Believe me, I've tried to slip hints, and even straight out told people that I needed help but no one heard me.

"I just about shit my pants. Give a guy a warning before you drop that little piece of information. I'm not one to pry but if you ever need to, um, talk... I'm here. It's scary out there, ya know? You need a friend and well, so do I. Plus there is no escaping me now, finders keepers," Evan jokes, blushing a bright red but he takes his eyes off the road to look at me.

He's serious. Even though the thought makes my palms sweat, I think I can trust him enough to let him in. One day at least but not today.

"Just drive, Obi-Wan Kenobi." I laugh as he beams at me, doing a little dance wiggle in his seat.

What a nerd. Maybe not all is bad in this fucked up world, one can only pray or take it into her own hands and fuck shit up. Here's to hoping I know what I'm doing and that it doesn't come back to bite me in the ass.

———

The moment Evan dropped me off, wishing me luck and exchanging numbers, I headed right for my room. Logan's car was in the driveway but I didn't see him or anyone else for that matter as I entered the house. Locking myself in my room sounded like a brilliant plan, so here I am after a shower. An hour later and clean from sticky soda, I sit in the middle of my bed and watch like a hawk for my bedroom door knob to start turning any second. I really am messed up in the head because I almost hope that Logan comes in here fuming. I want his anger as fucked up as that sounds. When he was fucking me, it was like he was putting all that rage into one place to focus and that focus was me. My gaze flickers to the bathroom door, making me shiver.

No. Guys like him feed on that power, once he has the girl, he'll take his fill then throw her to the side. That can't be me, no matter how tempting it is. Maybe I can find that somewhere else? I tried with trucker Adam but he didn't make the blackness disappear. Maybe I'm never meant to feel anything again, given one piece of heaven and that's all I deserve.

Tarnished. Exposed. Dirty.

That's how I feel day in and day out, my soul will never be clean again. No matter how much I scrub my skin, try to look different, be different... I'm still going to be Tillie. The girl who grew up in a motorcycle club of bad fucking people, raped by people who were supposed to live by the motto of having my back, blood in and blood out. I'm the girl who will always look over her shoulder, knowing that Cruz is always going to be one step behind even with hundreds of miles to separate us. I can't run from the past but I can accept my future even if it's dark skies.

Three rapid knocks at my door make me jump and dive for the knife under my pillow, hiding it behind my back. Diana pops her head in, her blonde bob straight and styled perfectly. You wouldn't think that this woman was a wreck for two whole days but here she is all put together and I hate that instantly. I know it's ridiculous but I don't want her to have this perfect life, safe behind her walls while I've only known true terror. It's not fair of me, but it's what I feel.

"Till. Why don't you come join us for dinner downstairs and get to know your stepfather and brother?" she says, smiling softly but it's the way her brown eyes crease at the corners that tells me I don't have a say in this matter.

She has to know what I went through back at the compound... She has to. I practically told her as much. Yet, she stands there in her nice clothes, pearl clutching neck-lace, and acts like everything is normal. Next, she'll be asking me to have tea with her out in the garden like the freaking queen. My stomach cramps, at least Lorrie wasn't pretending with me. She always showed her true colors even when they were ugly.

"Sure. I um, about the other day... I'm thankful, I really am, that you have taken me into your home. I'm not sure what you expect from me, not sure if I can be someone who you have pictured in your head. I'm damaged, the Demon Jokers made sure of tha-" She cuts me off by clearing her throat loudly and not staring at me, but somewhere over my shoulder.

"The past is the past, dear. No need to bring it up. You're here now and this gives me a chance to have the daughter I've never had. Now come along before dinner gets cold." She turns on her high heels, the sound of them clicking on the marble floor and down the staircase fades away as I sit there in disbelief.

How can she be that cold? I get that seeing your, what you thought was your dead daughter come back from the grave basically, can be a shock and hard to deal with but to dismiss my past like it's nothing... it leaves me feeling empty. I didn't want to talk about my time there, I just needed her to understand that I can't be what she wants.

I hear a door slam downstairs and quickly change into white Chanel sweats with a matching long sleeved crop top. Jesus. These designer clothes are the most comfortable things I've ever worn and the price tags on them make my heart race. I'm used to men throwing me money on stage but never would I have thought to waste money on clothes. It just really blows my mind. I do have an itch to dance, it's been almost a week. I hated the dancing on stage part with all the leering men but I didn't mind using the pole to dance with. It's a great way to see what the body can do and how much strength it takes. Maybe there's a studio or something I can go to, I need to release all my pent up anger and energy somehow. Lost in my thoughts, I've wandered down into the kitchen and don't see anyone until I keep walking and find the dining room.

A glossy oak table that seats twelve sits in the middle of the room with the dim lighting of a three tier chandelier hanging right over the middle of the table. Diana, I refuse to call her Mom, sits on the left side right next to Franco who sits at the head of the table like a man who rules over his household. Logan sits on his other side, glaring straight ahead. I think the only time I haven't seen him glare was when he was balls deep inside of me. My eyes roam around the table, trying to figure out where I should sit, maybe on the other end as far away from them.

"Sugar boo," Tey whispers in my ear from behind me, making me jump, "Come sit next to me. I promise I don't bite... much." The way his voice goes soft and raspy tells me that he has teeth and isn't afraid to use them.

Why do I like that?

He steps around me, brushing his arm against my shoulder, and goes to sit next to Logan, patting the seat beside him. Rolling my eyes, I take the offered chair and wait for something to happen. I've never had dinner with a family before, it was always just me and Uncle Rig eating at the picnic table outside on hot days in the Nevada heat. So far, I'm not impressed and maybe I didn't miss out on much. No one is talking. The only sounds are knives slicing perfectly through prime rib and closed mouth chewing.

Alrighty then.

"This looks really good. Must have taken a long time to cook." I tell Diana to break the awkward silence and ignore Logan choking on his drink just as he took a sip.

"Oh heavens no. I don't cook. A chef comes in three times a week and cooks all of our meals. I just have to preheat everything," she says, hardly touching her plate, and swirling her wine glass before taking a large swallow.

I honestly don't know how to respond so I decide to stuff my face instead. The prime rib melts in my mouth, a quiet moan slips past my lips as my eyes close in bliss. Fingers grasp the top part of my thigh causing my eyes to snap open and look down. I watch as long, strong fingers squeeze and slide over me until they grip the inside of my closed legs. Glancing up from under my lashes, I watch Tey as he continues to eat without looking at me while squeezing the inside of my thigh like he is giving me a massage. It feels so damned good. I shouldn't be feeling this way, shouldn't like it. Hell, his friend was just inside of me the other day. Why is he touching me?

My hand covers his in a death grip to make him stop before he heads further north. I almost choke to death on my food when he takes my hand quickly and places it right over his lap. His cock is hard, really hard, and I try to snatch my hand away without anyone noticing but he just tightens his fingers around mine.

"How was school, Tillie? The boys told me you made a new friend already and he was kind enough to drive you home," Franco suddenly says, my movements stall when he speaks, but I decide to squeeze Tey's cock in a painful grip as retaliation.

Looking directly into Franco's eyes, I feel my own widen when Tey's cock grows bigger and harder in the tight grip I have him in. I shouldn't be surprised, I already know Tey is crazy from the first time we met. I try to concentrate on Franco and what he asks until his words register in my mind. He's keeping tabs on me, which I expected nothing less but to throw it out there so casually tells me enough. He doesn't trust me.

"Yes. He was kind enough to give me a ride home. I didn't want to be a burden for you or your son." I lie between my teeth and sneak a glance at Logan to see him looking at my hand... which is kind of squeezing and stroking his friend's cock without meaning to.

When he glances up, it's with narrowed eyes but I can see his intense desire, enough that it causes my breath to catch and I become unbearably wet the longer he stares. What is with these men? Jesus, it's like I'm a virgin all over again and just found out how her body works with a man.

"Nonsense. They are happy to watch out for you. No more stranger car rides, Tillie, we are just trying to keep you safe," Franco says slowly, his dark brown eyes crinkle at the corners when I shift my gaze over to him, his smile stiff as he cuts into his meat all the while not looking away from me like he's imagining cutting me into tiny pieces.

It's hard to keep eye contact and I'm the first to break away, glancing down, pretending to act submissive. I'm startled to see my whole hand wrapped almost completely around the hard length of Tey's cock that's creeping down his thigh. I try to move my hand away from him again but his strong fingers over mine hold him tighter. I can't move even if I wanted to, the crazy fucker is practically moaning into his mashed potatoes at the painful grip. I eye the knife on the table, wondering if I can get away with stabbing him in a bloody mess and making a run for the door without getting caught. Deep in thought, I notice how quiet it is and look up to see everyone staring at me like they know just where my hand is under the table linen.

"Of course. I'm very grateful to you for looking out for me and welcoming me so kindly into your home." The sarcasm is clear in my voice, I escaped one prison and may have ended up in another without meaning to.

I need to leave, I don't even care if it's to a bench downtown in the cold and surrounded by other homeless people. It's better than being under these people's thumb, where they have you until your last dying breath. I'm not stupid, I know they are into some shady shit. It's evident in the way the guys hold themselves and seem to get away with just about anything. Hell, Dalton was getting a blowjob from a teacher, putting her in her place when I interrupted and she followed along with it. Everyone seems to give them a wide berth with wary caution. It's a look I know enough. People fear them and that will only lead to trouble for me, for fuck sakes Dalton is connected to another motorcycle club. It's only a matter of time before someone recognizes me or they sell me out. I don't even want to know what kind of business they are in, but I'm curious what Logan's dad does for a living. It just doesn't add up.

"We look after our own, maybe you can get to know your stepbrother and see the way we run the business. It would be just... delightful to have you in the fold. We're family after all." Franco shares a long look with Logan, communicating about something that I don't like.

Before I can ask what that business is, he clears his throat and places his napkin on the table to stand. Bending down, he kisses Diana on her cheek when she leans his way before rounding the table to stand behind my chair. The hairs on the back of my neck rise, I'm almost afraid to move. Diana doesn't look at me, she stares straight ahead drinking her wine. Franco places his hand on my shoulder, squeezing hard enough that I know the tender spot will be red, and I try to hide my wince at the simple touch. Darkness clouds at the edges of my vision, my breathing picks up and I know I'm about to have a panic attack. His voice, the only thing keeping the memories at bay, the threat clear as he speaks.

"If you try to fuck me over, I'll kill you," he whispers into my ear before straightening, and with one more squeeze that makes me wince, he lets go to address Logan and Tey. "Make sure she sees the way we run things around here boys and that she's... comfortable."

He leaves the room after that, the sound of clinking utensils making me dizzy. What the hell was that about? It's decided. I'm leaving tonight. I don't have a choice. It's be eaten alive in this cold fucking world or survive by dragging yourself out of your grave with teeth and nails.

I'm about to spiral into a memory that never leaves me and takes days to mentally escape. I've been threatened half my life by the Demon Jokers and now Franco. It never ends. I need air... to get away without raising suspicion. I flex my fingers, hoping Tey will let my hand go, but he just continues eating without noticing. I'll get him to notice and I don't care if Logan sees me threatening his friend with a steak knife. He just raises a dark eyebrow and waits to see what I'll do. Quickly, before I talk myself out of the consequences and the punishment that will surely follow, the knife is off the table and swiping across Tey's hand, barely missing the veins that bulge along his hand and up his arm.

His quiet hiss of pain makes me freeze, it's like my joints have locked in place and I'm just asking to get smacked around. The body is a fickle thing, your brain tells you one thing but the body doesn't always obey. At least he releases my hand. I dare to flicker my gaze up, preparing myself for the first hit. It's one you never forget. Only he's staring at the trail of blood pooling on top of his hand, watching it slide down his wrist. I expected a lot of things but the wide grin and pearly white teeth that make an appearance wasn't what I thought would happen.

"Tey, clear up your mess. Wouldn't want to get the white

tablecloth dirty," Logan casually orders from his slouched position in his chair, his gaze watching my pulse pound like crazy in my neck, and sliding his index finger back and forth over his plump sinful lips.

A chair screeches back from the table, heels clicking fast over the hardwood floors before the noise disappears. It could have been Diana but I wouldn't know because I'm busy staring into icy blue eyes framed by thick lashes, the color deepening a darker blue as Tey holds up his wrist to his mouth and slides out his surprisingly long tongue to lick up the trail of blood. I should be disgusted by his actions but the way he's staring at me like he wants to eat me alive, makes my stomach tighten with deep need and has me wishing he would make me bleed for him.

It's fucked up, I almost crave it.

I jump out of my chair so fast it goes crashing to the ground, but I hardly notice as my legs finally seem to be working, no longer frozen on the spot with fear, but with a desperation that makes me want to do very bad things.

"Aw, but it was just getting good. Come back, honey!" Tey yells, laughter following me out the archway.

"Sweet dreams, Tillie," Logan says softly in that deep raspy voice of his, but it sounds like a threat.

Making it to my room, I slam the door behind me and flick the lock into place before collapsing to the floor; hugging my stomach and breathing deeply through my mouth so I don't pass out. I need to plan how to leave without being noticed. I'm left with no other choice, I have to leave tonight before these guys decide to kill me just for fun. I'm done being threatened. Hurt. Used. There has to be somewhere out there for me to feel like my life isn't in danger.

Crawling across the room, I grab my duffle bag from the

closet and get to my feet to start throwing random clothing into it. It's only eight o'clock at night and I don't want to randomly make a break for the door now, I'll have to wait until everyone is asleep. Might as well try to get some shut-eye, who knows when I'll be able to rest once I'm on my own. Having to constantly look over my shoulder does get old but if it keeps me alive, I'll forever have a crick in my neck.

Placing my duffle bag by my feet, my body starts to feel like lead and my eyes become heavy, I collapse into the plush comforter that feels like fluffy clouds. My mind races with the possibles, memories trying to break to the surface, beating against me. Before I know it, I'm already drifting away, hopefully, into a place where no one can reach me.

CHAPTER 13

Tillie

"*R*un, Tillie. Keep running and don't look back or he'll catch up to you." Doris pushes against my shoulders and keeps pushing until I stumble back a step under the weight she uses against me. "You're going to die here. He's going to kill you, but not before he uses you first."*

Frantically, I turn on my hands and knees with gravel digging into my skin, scrambling to run away before hopping to my feet. I glance over my shoulder to tell her to run with me but she's gone. Looking forward, my shoes skid across the gravel and I fall on my butt with a thud as fear eats my insides alive.

Cruz stands there with his belt unbuckled and that curved hunting knife in his hand with blood smeared on the tip. I look down in horror at my legs which are covered with open wounds, raised scars of his name carved into my skin over and over again.

"I'll take and take until you beg me for death. Don't you know that dirty whores like yourself don't get to go to heaven? But don't

worry, I'll make sure that by the time I'm done with you, I'll be the God that you pray to." He reaches down for me, tearing at my clothes as I scream and scream for him to stop.

An ear piercing scream wakes me up, I'm disoriented from the nightmare but quickly collide with reality as I realize multiple hands are ripping off my clothes. I flail around, kicking and screaming for them to get off me as a knife slices through my pants and shirt, leaving me in my underwear and bra. It's dark in my room but there's enough light from the moon through my curtains to see four tall shadows towering over me, hidden from my eyes but I can see the outline of white on certain parts of their faces. The design of skeleton makeup on each face almost makes me piss my panties. My brain can't catch up fast enough with what is going on around me.

"Get the hell off of me! I'm not going back, you can't make me!" I yell at the skeleton faces surrounding me, tears running down my cheeks.

I'm flipped onto my stomach, and my hands and feet are quickly tied with rope hogtie style. I end up flopping around on the bed trying to get away before a bag is shoved over my head, the material sucking into my mouth with every panicked breath. I'm tossed over a broad shoulder, jostled around, and not one of them says a thing as I call them every curse word in the dictionary. I hear car doors open and suddenly I'm being thrown into the middle seat. From the size of them, I know my chance to run is long gone... the Demon Jokers have found me in no time at all. Two bodies squeeze in on either side of me, picking me up to place my head on one lap and legs on the other. The car starts, backing away from any freedom I thought I had and racing down the street, no doubt heading towards the compound.

It's so quiet, I can only hear my deep breathing and the vibration of the car under my stomach. With my dream still on the edge of my mind and now going back to that death trap, all the memories I try to shove down come back to haunt me like an old friend.

The night I was raped on that cold dirty cement floor, the carving of the big letters of Cruz's initials on my back, and the years by of being groped, violated, and never knowing when my time was coming to an end. The tears don't come anymore, my breathing picks up so much that it rattles my body as I lay as still as a statue. A hand smooths down my spine so lightly, the rough pad of their fingertips stop at the dimples of my back before sliding back up, the small nicks on his hand familiar of gun use. My pulse jumps, my nipples hardening into points through my bra and I curse my body at the pleasurable touch. I'd rather they make it hurt, I don't want to feel anything.

"I'll kill myself before you get that part of me ever again," I whisper the promise softly and let my body go lax under the continuing touch, deciding to save my strength for when I get out of this vehicle.

I'll go down fighting.

Time passes in a blur, my thoughts dark and dreadful. I can feel the driver cutting through lanes quickly, the smooth road has to be a highway with how easy the car moves. Lights flash through the hood, the burlap revealing nothing. Finally, we start to slow, making me wonder if they're just going to kill me here and now instead of delivering me to Cruz. Dumping my body over a bridge or in the ocean where I'll never be found. The driver slams on the brakes causing the car to stop abruptly. Someone throws the doors open, and a cool breeze makes my sweat slicked body shiver.

Hands grab my legs to drag me over the seats before flinging me to the ground, the rough asphalt scraping my side. The burlap is tugged off my head and the sudden brightness of the parking lot lights I'm lying under blinds me.

My head swivels left and right, taking in the rows of Ferraris in different colors, realizing I'm in a car dealership parking lot. The ropes digging into my wrists and ankles are cut away and before I can stand, a car engine purrs loudly to life behind me. Spinning around, I see two sets of matching grins behind skeleton makeup in the BMW i8 leaning out the passenger side of the car. Four familiar eyes look at my shivering, practically naked body huddled under the parking lot light.

"Sweet little bitch, you have... say about two minutes before the cops show up," Dalton says in a gruff voice, looking up and down my body with a wink.

Nicky sits in the front passenger seat and pulls a gun out, aiming right at me. I squeeze my eyes and pray it ends quickly. I thought I'd see a Joker on the other end of the gun but I guess fate has a twisted sense of humor. Five shots ring out rapidly, the sound of them hitting metal before I realize that the pain never comes. Peeking my eyes open, I see Nicky rolling his eyes and he stares straight ahead as if I'm not even here while gesturing to Logan to get going.

"Baby, I love how those booty shorts hug that ass. Can't wait to see it bouncing on my dick." Tey cocks his head to the side. "Can you hear that? Dalton, what's that sound like man?" He chuckles darkly, playing with his lip ring as he stares at the tattoo on my hip.

"Sounds like the cops. Better hurry!" Dalton snickers, snapping his teeth at me.

The skeleton makeup design really gives them the image

of death, the hollowed cheekbones, the way it makes their gazes stand out against the black smudging around the eyelids.

"We shall see who makes it back home first," Logan taunts from the driver's seat, leaning around Nicky with a smug grin.

He punches the gas without waiting for an answer from me, the tires leave skid marks on the pavement and it's suddenly just me stranded in the lot. When I turn around, it's to see three Ferraris dented in bullet holes and broken windows.

Those motherfuckers left me for bait. I can't have the cops catch me, I'll go to jail and Payne will find me in no time. He has eyes and ears everywhere, the system doesn't stop him. The sound of sirens gets louder and I say fuck it. My chest heaves as I glance around frantically until I spot a black Ferrari F8 Spider inside the dealership building and run barefoot across the parking lot. It's not like I have a crowbar or my knife to mess with the wires to start a car. With no other choice, I grab the largest rock of their display outside the windows, grunting under the weight, and toss it at the glass window. It shatters into tiny pieces and a loud blaring alarm starts up the moment the rock makes contact with the glass. If the cops weren't coming before, they are now. I grind my teeth as I step onto the shards, blocking out the pain and the bloody footprints I'm leaving behind. My running limp is pathetic as I hurry over to the flashy sports car. The driver's door opens easily because of course, they don't lock them up inside. Rolling my eyes, I quickly jog over to the receptionist's area and see the keys I'm looking for on a hook under the desk. Do they think because it's a high brand of a vehicle that no one would dare break in? Guess so.

I climb onto the driver's seat, I take a moment to admire the sleek leather material under my panty-clad ass, the smooth wheel my hands slide over. Key in the ignition, it roars to life like a beast and I'm spinning the car in seconds in a one eighty with burning rubber and smoke. Deciding not to pull a Dukes of Hazard because I do have some class, I burst through the already shattered glass floor to ceiling window. The car jumps over a small curb, a sound like crushed metal reaches my ears and it causes me to grimace in pain for the Ferrari.

Just as I'm racing out of the lot, the flashing blue and red lights peel around the corner, picking up speed to chase after me. Throwing the clutch down and stomping my bloody foot on the gas, my teeth grind at the pain but it's forgotten as I'm pushed into the seat and the car shoots forward. The way this car moves between the few vehicles on the back roads is a dream. It's like sailing over water, just above the surface. The siren of the two cop cars behind me get louder, gaining up on my rear, closer and closer. I switch over into oncoming traffic, barely missing plowing into a truck, and sideswiping a few cars that are parallel parked on the road with sparks flying.

"Shit. Come on, come on!" I grunt out, shifting gears again to pick up speed once I'm back on the right side of the road.

Los Angeles is like one big maze, I hardly know the way back to Logan's but luckily there are freaking signs everywhere that lead me right to Beverly Hills. It's probably for the best if I stay off the highway, considering it's a one way and I'll eventually get caught. A carefree laugh bursts out of my mouth when I glance in the rearview mirror and see the cops fading in the distance. The Ferrari is too fast for them to catch up and for some reason, I'm laughing so hard that tears form in my eyes. One second I'm whooping and cheering at the risk, the way I outran the cops, and then the next second I'm a woman possessed. I'm angry... no, I'm livid.

How dare they? To so carelessly leave me out there in my underwear and to take the fall for their actions... I'm out for blood. Time flies when you're driving like your life depends on it, the city lights flashing by so fast that they are a blur, and then all of a sudden you're in a quiet neighborhood with everyone's perfect lawns, perfect families, and perfect lives. I don't care if the Ferrari is waking the whole neighborhood up or how the bumper is probably dragging against the ground, scratches up and down the vehicle... I want my piece of flesh before I leave California far behind me.

The gates are wide open when I pull up to Logan's house, so I speed up the long driveway and come to a quick stop with the tires screeching. I throw the door open with the keys still in the ignition, and limp over to the open garage door where laughter is coming from. I'll worry about the pain I'm in later, right now, I want to cause pain to someone else. The first person who comes into view is Logan and I don't think, my body just reacts. With a scream of frustration and hate, I run at him, my fists flying, looking for any body part that I can reach and will cause harm.

"You fucking cocksucker! You guys left me for the cops! What kind of asshol-" I'm ripped away from Logan, kicking and scratching at any exposed skin I can get to until a cell-phone is thrust into my face with a video playing.

It takes me a second to get past the red haze that I'm trapped in to understand what's happening.

"This, my darling, would be called blackmail," Nicky

states, coming into view with his cold emerald eyes pinning me into place.

I slump in Tey's arms with confusion clouding my brain, absentmindedly noticing it's him swaying us both by the small cut on the back of his hand that's placed over my stomach.

"Blackmail? I don't...what?" I continue watching the video of me breaking into the dealership and hijacking the Ferrari like a car thief, some dirtbag criminal doped up on drugs.

Only a crazy person would steal a car in their underwear. I was set up just so they could get blackmail on me?

"You wouldn't want this plastered all over the news stations, would you? Takes only one phone call to have the cops here in minutes and the Demon Jokers to find out where their missing princess is," Nicky threatens softly and deadly, his plan all too clear now.

I'm a pawn in a game I can't win. He puts his phone away and steps back, crossing his arms over his broad chest.

"No," I whisper brokenly, feeling lost.

"Yes," Tey taunts in my ear darkly, using that wicked tongue of his to lick the shell of my ear, his tongue ring giving me shivers before he bites down hard on the tender flesh.

"We own you from here on out," Logan states, his pupils expand with the possessive look he gives me.

"To do what we want with." Dalton finishes for Logan, reaching out to grab a lock of my hair, and twirling it around his finger.

I smack his hand away and buck against Tey's body in an attempt to break free but it just causes him to groan in pleasure with how much I'm wriggling against him.

"Get on your knees," Logan demands smoothly like

whiskey over ice, his lips set in a firm line and his honeyed eyes watching me, just waiting for me to fight.

Tey adds a little pressure on my shoulders to push me along, and I debate under the weight of my odds of ever really leaving this lifestyle behind. I ran from a motorcycle club into the arms of another crew of criminals.

"I hate you," I say with so much passion I almost believe it myself, convincing my body to tag along is another story.

"I don't care. You see when your father is the Chief of police you get away with some crime, but when that man turns into something so powerful even the city is scared of him, you get away with everything." Logan nods his head at Nicky and Tey over my shoulder, both of them coming to my side and pushing me down until my knees smack against the epoxy garage floor.

"You're the fucking mafia?!" I hiss out, Logan's image getting dizzy until the pain on my scalp brings me back as he pulls my head back by my hair.

"Mafia, meth makers, drug dealers, criminals... call it whatever you want. You're in our world now, baby girl. Now be a good girl and do as you're told." He grips my hair tighter, and my neck starts to ache from the strain but my betraying body loves it.

My breathing picks up, my skin flushed, and my nipples strain against the lace of my bra. The sound of a zipper brings back a memory of that night, I can almost feel the basement's dirty floor scraping against my back as a Joker ripped through my virginity.

"Little bitch, we really gotta stop meeting like this," Dalton smirks, his thumb brushing back and forth over my parted lips as I stare up at him in a daze. "Open wide, let's see those skills you bragged about."

How wrong I was when I thought his cock was huge

before in his teacher's mouth, it's even bigger without a mouth wrapped around him. It wouldn't be the first time a blowjob was forced on me but it would be the first time my pussy gets dripping wet just thinking about it. Dalton steps closer until it's only him I can see. He taps the large mushroom head of his cock against my lips and I can't help but peek up at him from under my lashes. He's already staring at me with a lopsided smirk like he knows what I'm thinking.

"If you bite me, I'll rip out your teeth until it's a smooth ride for my cock," he threatens with a deep chuckle, smiling in delight when I try struggling out of Tey and Nicky's grip.

Without warning, he plunges past my lips, the wide girth stretching my mouth and already making my jaw ache. The fist in my hair doesn't loosen, nor the rough slide in and out of my mouth, it's enough to make my eyes water.

"Look at her taking my cock around those wide, pink lips. I knew you could, little bitch." Dalton groans, his thumbs hooking into the sides of my mouth to stretch it wider.

I gag when he reaches the back of my throat, tears leaking down my cheeks but I keep going even as I glare up at him.

"That's enough," Logan orders, shoving Dalton away before he can finish, and I breathe deeply in rough pants as I watch him zip up his pants.

I think it's over when the guys let go of my shoulders but the cruel smirk gracing Dalton's wide lips stops me from getting off my knees.

"In my kingdom, you do as I say and when I say," Logan says in a deep voice, his hand in my hair pulling harder until it stings my scalp and I'm looking upside down at him.

A shocked gasp leaves my lips when I'm smacked on the

side of my cheek with one of the guys' cock. It's crude and nasty but that doesn't stop them from making me feel little, to show them exactly where my place is and I loathe how damp my panties are. My nostrils flare and my eyes hurt from holding in angry tears as one lone thick finger slips into my underwear, sliding between my wet folds back and forth so slowly, to prove how wet my pussy is for them. I'm ashamed of my reaction but I can't control it. Not being able to see who's touching me with the way Logan has me in his hold, the need to plead them to keep going climbs up my throat but the finger circling my clit disappears just when I was about to break. Judging by the drawn out groan and the deep inhale I hear, Tey, the psycho, was the one touching me. I pretend the sucking sound with a slight pop and another groan of agony doesn't make my pussy clench with need, or that he was just sucking his finger with the taste of me on it.

Glaring up at Logan, his honey eyes mock me and he shoves my head back down to receive the rest of my punishment. Nicky stands in front of me, his green eyes hypnotizing and a whole lot of scary behind the skeleton makeup. I can hear their voices loud and clear but when I look at them, I feel disoriented like I'm really not here and I've made it to hell. Maybe I never really left the compound but that thought goes flying out the window as I feel enough pain to tell me it's real. The cold floor bruises my knees, the tight grip in my hair restraining me, and the eight inches of thick cock sliding past my lips again... pain and pleasure blend together. My eyes widen in shock, seeing from base to tip tattoos around the whole length of his cock and I wonder if the rest of the hidden parts of his body is covered in art too.

"I think she likes it. Do you like sucking my cock, Tillie?"

Nicky asks darkly with his eyes glaring at me when I remain silent, continuing to lick him around the head that leaks pre cum before going back down on him again.

He slaps my cheek, enough to lightly sting and the pain causes me to choke around his cock as he shoves down my throat in a fast hammering movement that will no doubt bruise and leave me with a raspy voice.

"Answer him," Logan demands, shoving my face forward until my nose brushes against the exposed skin of Nicky's abs and the sharp V of his hips.

He releases me after a moment so I can breathe. I gasp for breath like it's my last and watch through watery eyes when Nicky steps away without coming too. Not being able to see the lust, greed, and possession in their eyes, I close my own and admit something that I wish was a lie.

"Yes." My voice sounds hollow to my own ears, defeated.

"Good girl," Logan whispers for my ears only but it makes my eyes snap open in shock at the praise. He starts talking to Tey in a louder voice and circles around to gaze down at my pathetic self at their feet. "I've already had a piece of her and I have to say she really begged for it, but don't they all? Tey, you want a turn, brother?" Logan offers his friend like I'm a prized possession, an object.

I hate him. I hate them. I hate the way my body craves all the things it's been missing. I hate the wet gush between my thighs each time one of them touches me. Maybe I wasn't made to run away from my problems but face them head on. Tey crouches over to my side, moving the hair away from my wet stained face, and traces his finger over my feather tattoo hiding the raised bumps of the letter C.

"No. I'll wait until she's so desperate that she's begging me to make her bleed. What can I say? I love them crazy."

Tey shrugs and leans forward to lick my cheek, right over the tears that escaped.

He stands suddenly after looking at me for a long minute like he was searching for something in my gaze and walks over to Nicky's side. All four of them loom over me now, staring down at me in a way that makes my very existence feel very small, almost as if I'm a nobody and not one person would care if I never showed my face again.

"Play by the rules, Tillie, and maybe you won't die. By the time we are done with you, marking you in every way possible... you'll end up begging for death. Or you could surprise me and live. Only time will tell. Let the games begin." My heart pounds, wanting to escape my ribcage as Logan delivers that message with a devilish smirk and walks into the house without a backwards glance.

The guys follow after him, not one of them saying anything until it's just me, kneeling on the ground where I always feel like I belong. It started just like this for me in the basement and it seems to be an endless cycle, maybe one of these days I won't be able to get back up. A shiver wracks my body, a cold empty feeling gripping me tight. It confused me for a moment when they each took a turn using me, withholding from coming down my throat or marking me. They wanted to show what kind of power they have over me, that I'm to be used whenever one of them feels like it. It really is a game to them and I'm sick of being an object to be used over and over again. Something inside of me crawls its way up my stomach until it's burning in my chest... pure fucking rage.

I didn't run away just to slowly die for some controlling, asshole punks. Doris once told me that one day I'm going to fly so high that no one can touch me and that's exactly what I'm going to do. There on the cold garage floor, cheeks stained with dried tears, I make a promise to myself. No more hiding. No more running. No more fearing those higher up on the food chain. I'm taking what's mine by the balls even if it does end up killing me.

I'll show them all that they are messing with the wrong spiteful girl.

EPILOGUE

Cruz

*I*f you take enough of a deep inhale, you'll still be able to smell rotting corpses that have been buried in freshly turned soil and the faint stale taste of copper in the air after so many years of use. This right here is my favorite place, it holds many memories for me but the one that sticks is the night I received my patch. Climbed up the ladder as her screams echoed around this basement, still so fresh in my mind.

Inhale, exhale.

Just closing my eyes, I can see her laying on the floor, screaming for it all to stop, but the moment my blade carved her up so prettily is when she became silent. Now she's gone out of my reach and I can't feel ecstasy coursing through my veins no matter how many people I kill. She's the only blood I want, the only cunt that will satisfy my thirst.

Finally, fucking finally, I'm getting closer to having her back. I'll have her exactly where I want her soon enough.

She's mine, all mine. Searching for the rat didn't take long. Spike sang like a canary and I cut out his tongue after. Couldn't stand the whiny prospect's voice as he pleaded for mercy. I can say his body decomposing in the lone chair right by the basement stairs is a nice message to anyone who dares to think about crossing us. Now, the real fun begins. It doesn't give me that certain high, but it's enough to last me over until Tillie is on her back and craving my blade.

"Doris. Poor, poor Doris. Aren't you tired yet? Have you had enough? Just tell me what I want to know and it can all stop. Payne will forgive you over time." The lies come easily off my tongue, Payne would rather see this bitch dead.

Luckily, he told me to do whatever it takes, it almost makes me giddy with glee. When Spike told me he was the one to let her out of the compound, I saw red. It took a lot of restraint to not gut him and watch his insides spill out. He just had to whisper one name who helped her escape and now here we are. Doris hasn't admitted anything, she's a stubborn whore who's been here long enough that she knows how to stay silent.

"Where is she? Just tell me where, Doris, and I'll bring her home nice and safe." She stares down at her lap, her blonde hair laying in dirty strands in her face as she pants for breath.

I have to say, I'm impressed. She hasn't broken yet, but she will. Even if she's tied down to this chair for days, I will rip off her toenails on the other foot. I tried to scare her with rape, I brought in some of the club members but this bitch has been a sweetbutt since before I was born. She's not going to break with a threat of a fuck. She's probably seen more than I have over the years. So I've resorted to torture; slashes from my blade make rivers of her blood pool at the bottom of her feet, and the tattoo on her arm is gone as I skinned that off. It might come in handy, maybe I'll send it to Tillie once I find out where she is. A nice little present.

Growing impatient, I bend down in front of her and swiftly stab her thigh, the blade sinking deep. Her scream makes my eyes roll in the back of my head, high on the pain and I can't wait to give her more.

"I could do this all day, Doris. Have you ever wondered what it would feel like to have a knife shoved so far up your pussy that you bleed slowly to death as your insides are rearranged? I can show you." I can make good on that promise, the excitement is clear in my voice as I threaten her.

She pants, her one eye that isn't swollen shut cracking open to stare at me with pure panic. A shiver works down my spine. This is it.

I'm coming for you, Tillie.

"S-sh-she's with h-her mom," Doris whispers brokenly, her head dropping to her chest as she sobs.

I tilt my head, confused because no way does Lorrie have the cunt in hiding. She hates Tillie, never claimed her as her own daughter. A slow grin spreads across my face as a thought clicks... unless, oh this is too good.

I think Payne and I need to have a little chat.

Tillie is mine. She's mine and she's going to die by my blade after I teach her a lesson for thinking she can hide from me.

No one leaves me. No one. I'm all she needs, all she wants!

To be continued

AFTERWORD

So... how are we doing? You okay? What a cliffy, am I right or what?

Fear not, book two is already in the works! Coming soon in 2021!

Now that you're done panicking (You're still freaking out aren't you?), I just want to thank you for reading my dark romance. It's been stuck in my head for a while and I'm glad to see the characters come alive. Just wait until book two... you have no idea... no idea what's in store for you!

I want to thank Penn Cassidy, my bestie from far away, I couldn't have done this without you. Constantly cheering me on and listening to all my bitching about my characters acting up. You're amazeballs and I couldn't ask for a better friend/co-writer! Much love girl. Crystal Partin, thank you so much for reading and helping me with these punks. Your input helped so much. Polly, the way you edit... I'm keeping you. You don't have a choice, sorry not sorry. Emma, I'm so glad you were along with this crazy ride and proofreading my psychos!

Thank you readers for diving in and I hope you loved this book as much as I do. Tillie has grown so much, never giving up and being a badass even when the guys put her down. Follow any of my links to stay updated on book two and future works. Thank you so much from the bottom of my heart.

If you love/hate this story, please consider leaving a review. Regarding spelling/grammar, feel free to reach out to me in one of the following links below or if you just want to talk about Spiteful Punks. Thank you.

STALKING LINKS FOR MADELINE FAY

Facebook Group:
https://www.facebook.com/groups/270252770540820/

Newsletter: https://www.subscribepage.com/MadelineFayNL

Facebook like page: https://www.facebook.com/madelinefayauthor/

Instagram: http://Instagram.com/Madelinefay_author/

ABOUT MADELINE FAY

Madeline lives in rural Michigan in a castle with all her fur babies and husband. She loves to read, you'll find her in her tower with her kindle and cup of tea. She has a few addictions, chocolate is her weakness and anything seventies related. She's a hippy at heart. She has an evil day job, but at night she watches over her city in the shadows and calls herself Batman. Not really but she keeps hoping it might come true one day. She's in her bat cave writing and plotting mad, evil genius, stories while sipping some wine.

Made in the USA
Columbia, SC
05 April 2021

35099986R00114